Death Is a Bargain

**Center Point
Large Print**

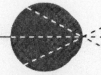

**This Large Print Book carries the
Seal of Approval of N.A.V.H.**

Death Is a Bargain

NORA CHARLES

CENTER POINT PUBLISHING
THORNDIKE, MAINE

This Center Point Large Print edition
is published in the year 2006 by arrangement with
The Berkley Publishing Group, a division of Random House, Inc.

The text of this Large Print edition is unabridged. In other
aspects, this book may vary from the original edition.
Printed in the United States of America.
Set in 16-point Times New Roman type.

ISBN 1-58547-677-3

Library of Congress Cataloging-in-Publication Data

Charles, Nora.
    Death is a bargain / Nora Charles.--Center Point large print ed.
        p. cm.
    ISBN 1-58547-677-3 (lib. bdg. : alk. paper)
      1. Large type books. I. Title.

PS3573.A42116D425 2005
813'.54--dc22

2005016091

To the memory of Ray

Acknowledgments

IN WASHINGTON, D.C.—
My deepest gratitude to Peggy Hanson for her generous gift of time and editing talent.

Thanks to Cordelia Benedict and Peggy Hanson for being the book's first readers during our literary lunches at the Smithsonian.

Thanks to Steve Smith for his advice and support.

Thanks to Pat Sanders and Dr. Diane Shrier for our Sunday morning walks and talks.

Thanks to my critique colleagues, the Rector Lane Irregulars: Donna Andrews, Carla Coupe, Ellen Crosby, Laura Durham, Peggy Hanson, Valerie Patterson, and Sandi Wilson.

Thanks to Lynda Hill, Patrick Hyde, Audrey Liebross, Bonner Menking, Jennifer Pfalzgraf, and Mimi Tandler for their fast, last-hurrah edits.

IN SOUTH FLORIDA—
Thanks to Gloria and Paul Stuart: dear friends, gracious hosts, talented researchers, and great promoters.

Thanks to Diane and Dave Dufour, my longtime friends and supporters.

Thanks to Joyce Sweeney, a wonderful author and my mentor.

IN NEW YORK AND NEW JERSEY—
Thanks to Doris Holland for being there for over forty years.

Thanks to my son, Billy, who listens, even when he's heard it before.

And, finally, thanks to my editor, Tom Colgan, and my agent, Peter Rubie; without them no one would know Kate Kennedy.

Death Is a Bargain

One

A midget in a tuxedo swung on a trapeze, missing the outstretched arms of a blonde in a bejeweled leotard. The blonde hung by her heels in mid-air. The midget fell fifty feet into a classic red Volkswagen convertible. Kate Kennedy hoped the car was well-padded.

Scrambling out of the Bug's backseat, followed by three full-size clowns, the midget yelled to the cheering crowd, "Welcome to the second-greatest show on earth."

"Only in South Florida," Kate whispered to her dead husband, Charlie, wishing he was with her, feeling for a fleeting moment almost as if he were.

"The ringmaster's cute, isn't he?" Marlene Friedman, Kate's former sister-in-law and best friend since childhood, grinned. "I once had a fling with a Barnum and Bailey midget. In Sarasota, at their training grounds, the winter of 'sixty-two, I think—anyway, after I divorced Walter, but before I married Kevin."

After more than sixty years of girl talk, Marlene could still surprise Kate.

They'd been checking out the mile-square Palmetto Beach flea market, scouting out the best available space to sell Marlene's "treasures" or "junk"—the description depending on which one of them was talking. Kate allowed that a shocking-pink hula hoop circa 1957 might qualify in either category. But both agreed that things had taken over Marlene's condo.

11

Since Marlene had been stopping at every table to shop instead of making any attempt to select a site, Kate suggested they get out of the relentless April midday sunshine, grab a hot dog, and watch the free two o'clock performance of the famous Cunningham Circus located in a center ring, complete with a big top, smack in the middle of the flea market.

It might not be the second-greatest show on earth, but when two elephants, wearing pink boas, lined up and danced—"As good as the Radio City Rockettes," according to the ringmaster—Kate was enjoying herself so much that she sprang for a second round of hot dogs and two more orders of truly greasy, totally delicious French fries.

Marlene laughed. "I hope you brought your Pepcid AC."

"I never leave home without it." Kate shook her head. Her digestive system, like the rest of her, wasn't what it used to be.

The elephant trainer, a perky little brunette dressed in a royal-blue drum majorette costume, wielded her baton to prod one of the elephants, poking the animal with more force than Kate deemed necessary.

Her half-eaten French fry lost its flavor. An image of her beloved Westie, Ballou, home alone, popped into her head. Kate might be overly squeamish, but her delight dissipated, replaced by a vague, nagging concern for animals. Those in the circus might be mistreated. Was she neglecting Ballou by leaving him alone?

She felt relieved when, to the roar of the cheering crowd, "the second-greatest show on earth" came to an end.

"Marlene, is that you, my girl?" They were stalled at the end of a long line trying to exit the Big Top when a clown—Kate thought he'd been the third one out of the Volkswagen—came up behind them and enveloped Marlene in a bear hug.

"Hello, Sean." Marlene attempted to poke her head around his wild red wig and funny hat, getting grease-paint on her cheek. "Kate, say hello to Sean Cunningham. Sean, this is Kate Kennedy, my best friend and sister-in-law."

Marlene never added the qualifying "former" when explaining their kinship. Somehow, that pleased Kate.

"Charmed, I'm sure." The wiry little man spoke in a soft, lilting, not-quite-a-brogue voice. He removed a huge glove, then awkwardly twisted around to shake Kate's hand. His oversize shoes were firmly planted against the outside of Marlene's sandals, making it impossible for her to move.

Where had Marlene met this clown?

"Do you dance, Kate?" The lilt lingered. Irish born? Or an affected accent?

"We met at Ireland's Inn." Marlene squirmed, trying to get free of his feet. "Back off, Sean. I can't breathe."

"Sorry, my pet." Sean two-stepped in reverse, almost knocking Kate over. How did he walk in those clod-hoppers?

"Ah, yes. Ireland's Inn. Great music there. I'm what you might call a regular. On more than one happy occasion, Marlene and I have shared a slow dance and a wee drink." Sean winked at Kate. "You'll have to stop by sometime. I do a mean cha-cha."

"I don't dance." Kate lied, sounding cold and convincing.

Marlene glared at her.

Sean, seemingly unfazed, smiled. "What brings you two lovely ladies to the circus?"

"Junk." Marlene laughed. "We're looking for a table or a booth in the flea market where I can get rid of mine. But I'm a junkie, so I kept buying, until Kate dragged me to the matinee."

"Admitting your addiction is the first step." Kate, guilty as charged of compulsive neatness, felt her sister-in-law had just made a major breakthrough.

"Yes, I guess I'm ready." Marlene sighed, then licked her lower lip. "Say, Sean do you know of a good location?"

"It would be my great pleasure to assist you. Why, I have the perfect spot in mind, don't I?" Sean, not without difficulty, turned full circle, aiming his big shoes toward the exit. "Follow me, girls."

Any illusion of glamour had vanished with the human and animal performers. The center ring, shorn of fancy costumes and colorful banners, looked gray and grimy.

With the stadium-style seats empty, the smell of manure trumped the odors of half-eaten hot dogs, crumpled, grease-stained containers, and the remnants of relish, mustard, and stray pieces of popcorn littering the dirt floor.

From behind a red velvet curtain, Kate heard a muffled moan. Could it be the elephant the trainer had prodded? Or had she only imagined the sound?

She tripped over a crushed Coke can and, though the open space was vast, felt trapped. She'd never forgotten *I Love You Honey, But the Season's Over*, a book she'd read decades ago, chronicling a small-town girl's doomed love affair with a handsome, itinerant circus performer.

To escape the big top—this very minute—Kate Kennedy would have followed Sean Cunningham to Hell.

Two

Compared to what Kate had seen of the rest of the flea market, the spot Sean led them to seemed like heaven.

They'd exited into a clean corridor under an air-conditioned, canopied tent only steps away from the circus. The air felt crisp and comfortable, motivating the, though junk-food fed, well-entertained circus patrons to stop and buy from the vendors.

The setting may have improved; however, the clown's deteriorating appearance had gone from distasteful to disgusting. Makeup had caked in the deep creases on his cheeks and when he wiped his still sweaty—despite the burst of cold air—forehead, he removed most of his left eyebrow and stained the back of his right hand.

Kate tried not to recoil, reminding herself that first impressions can be misleading, that Sean was probably a fine man, and that she was too damn fussy and fastidious for her own good.

Her upset stomach, its level of acidity a strange but often accurate harbinger of trouble, suggested a different scenario.

Could the cause of her distress be the empty table?

Six tables/booths were positioned, three on each side of the busy corridor. Five were drawing long lines of customers, so dense that Kate couldn't see the vendors. One table was barren, its metal top exposed and ugly in its nakedness. No merchandise. No seller. No buyers.

"Prime space." Sean pointed to eager shoppers, still queuing up. "Hundreds of folks pass through here every day on their way to and from our circus." He sounded proud of the family business.

"The location manager never mentioned this area." Marlene beamed, seeing the same dollar signs as Kate.

"He's not a Cunningham, is he?" Sean yanked a large, none-too-clean handkerchief from a deep pocket in his roomy plaid pants and took another swipe at the greasepaint. His face now resembled a Dalí painting. "We decide which vendors work the corridors off the circus."

Beware of clowns bearing gifts. Kate's stomach lurched anew.

"The Dewars guy died Sunday night." Sean jerked a

thumb at the bare table. "We removed his shelves and packed up his wares yesterday. A great loss. We're all going to the service on Thursday. Both the corridor and the circus will be closed in honor of our very own Whitey Ford. His real name was Bob, but his nickname was a no-brainer; he looked just like the Yankee pitcher. Same blond hair. Same slim frame. And, funny enough, Whitey had the largest collection of Dewars pitchers in the country."

"How did Whitey die?" Kate remembered the real Whitey Ford pitching a no-hitter decades ago at Yankee Stadium, while Charlie had cheered so loudly he'd lost his voice.

"According to the cop who called me, he'd been lounging in the bathtub watching a *Seinfeld* rerun. The TV fell in the tub." Sean shrugged. "Curtains."

"An accident?" Marlene ran her hand across the scarred metal table.

"Yeah." Sean nodded. "An accident."

Kate found his nod oddly eager, like a naughty puppy looking for approval.

"Whitey had been drinking. The cops found a pitcher half-filled with scotch and an empty glass on the top of the hamper next to the TV."

Kate had read the story—buried on the bottom of page four in this morning's *Sun-Sentinel*—just a few lines about a man with no family dying at home alone. Nothing about Bob Ford's Yankee nickname. Nothing about his passion for Dewars pitchers. Nothing about his booth in the flea market.

"Let's go over to the office and sign the lease." Sean grabbed Marlene's elbow. "By the time we get you all set up, the matinee crowd will be gone, and I'll introduce you to the ladies and gentlemen of the corridor."

"Sean, wait up!" A high-pitched voice stopped their slow procession toward the tent's flap.

The young animal trainer—she appeared to be about twenty, the same age as Kate's oldest granddaughter—had changed from her blue satin majorette outfit into jeans and a tight black T-shirt with requisite midriff exposure, and was weaving her way to Sean's side.

"Donnie, what do you want?" Under the grotesquely smeared make-up, Kate watched Sean's face light up. No fool like an old clown.

The girl thrust a damp towel and a jar of cold cream at Sean.

"Clean your face, Mr. C, or these ladies will be embarrassed to be seen with you." She smiled, showing small, even, white teeth, and held out a hand to Kate. "I'm Donna Viera, ma'am, pleased to meet you."

And Sean calls you Donnie, Kate thought. Before she could respond either with a handshake or a greeting, the girl had moved on to Marlene.

"Mrs. Kate Kennedy and Ms. Marlene Friedman," Sean paused, as if seeking approval from Marlene for remembering to call her Ms. Score one for the clown. Marlene so disliked being addressed as Mrs. or, God forbid, Miss. "Say hello to South Florida's finest animal trainer."

Kate started as Marlene shook hands with "South Florida's finest animal trainer."

"What's wrong, Mrs. Kennedy?" Though Donna's tone conveyed concern, her navy blue eyes were cold.

Should Kate wave a red flag? Why not? She'd discovered one of the true joys of growing older was the ability to speak her mind and damn the consequences. "I was thinking about a cry I heard just before we left the circus. It sounded like an elephant moaning."

"You have good ears, Mrs. Kennedy." Donna's eyes flashed. "Edna, our youngest dancer, had a thorn stuck under her big toe. I removed it right after the show. She did moan a bit, I'm afraid."

"No anesthesia, I gather." Even to herself, Kate sounded like a prosecutor.

Donna laughed. It sounded cold. "Would you use anesthesia to remove a splinter, Mrs. Kennedy?"

Knowing when to fold, Kate said, "Only a local on my son, Kevin. Though he grew up to be a firefighter, he hated to have a splinter removed. I guess nursing a frightened child has left me overly sympathetic."

"Well, if you like, I can arrange for you to visit the patient." Snide, Kate thought.

"Yes, thank you. I'd love to." Kate kept smiling. "Maybe when we return from signing our lease."

"Maybe tomorrow, Mrs. Kennedy." Again Donna's dark eyes belied the lightness of her words. "I still have to groom the animals. And we have another show tonight at seven-thirty."

"Then we're off, ladies." Sean had cleaned up, his

naked face a pudgy mass of freckles, wrinkles, and jowls. "They close the office at five."

"Whoa," Donna said. "Are these ladies taking over Whitey Ford's spot?"

"Well, yes." Kate thought she heard a quiver in Sean's voice. Why would an employer be afraid of an employee?

"You can't even wait until the body's cold to turn a profit, can you?" Donna grabbed the dirty towel and the cold cream jar. "Shame on you, Sean Cunningham. You're no better than a ghoul!"

Three

While Sean had appeared intimidated by Donna Viera, the Palmetto Beach Flea Market's location manager, a Hobbit-like middle-aged man, fawned over Sean. His many variations of "Yes, sir, Mr. Cunningham," took pandering to a new low. As Marlene signed the "special-conditions"—short term, low rent—lease, Kate wondered if the Cunningham family owned a controlling share of the flea market as well as the circus.

The small, ordinary business procedure, with handshakes all around, capped with Marlene's flowery Palmer Method–style signature, stirred up memories of Charlie, who'd died clutching the pen he'd used to close on their Ocean Vista condo.

A heart attack. Alive one moment, gone the next. And a big chunk of Kate's heart had gone missing, too. Oh, she could feel emotion. She fiercely loved her two sons, adored her two beautiful granddaughters and her dearest friend, Marlene. She even, if in a more limited fashion, loved her daughter-in-law, Jennifer. But romance—any semblance of real passion—had died with Charlie. After almost a year, that void still hurt.

Walking back from the shoddy trailer that served as the flea market's office to Marlene's and her new place of business, Kate felt a sense of excitement. A poor substitute for passion, yet the spark tingled. She hadn't held a job for over forty years, not since she'd flown as a stewardess for the long-defunct Eastern Airlines. She and Marlene had agreed that thirty percent of the profit would be hers. She couldn't wait to get to work. Or to get out of the oppressive heat and humidity.

The South Florida sun, even at five-thirty, remained strong. Kate, so fair-skinned she always wore 40-plus sunscreen, pulled the brim of her soft straw hat down over her ears, and stared at the scorched-to-brown grass.

But what a day. They'd driven into the flea market under a bright yellow arch reminiscent of a supersized McDonald's. The entrance, located off Neptune Boulevard several miles west of I-95, led into a field of crisp green grass, thick and trimmed. At 9:45 A.M., their receipt, marked "642," indicated that 641 cars, with God only knows how many passengers, had beaten them to market.

The outdoor tables closest to the arch and the parking

lots sold pretty things: flowering plants, their blooms a riot of hot pink and purple. Hand-painted, ceramic Chinese garden seats. Antique—or created to look antique—Chinese fish pots. White enamel rocking chairs and small end tables, designed to remind the buyers of furniture once found on grandma's front porch. Everything reflected the shabby chic so popular in the late nineties and remaining in demand at this flea market.

A wide-striped canvas deck chair had caught Kate's attention, flooding her with memories of long-ago lazy summers and the blue and white horizontal stripes on the chaise-like beach chair her father had set up every Saturday morning on the sand at Rockaway Beach more than half a century ago.

Marlene, seemingly enchanted by the array of merchandise, had said, "Shouldn't we get a table here?"

Kate had asked and learned that these vendors parked their vans in the lot nearest the entrance. They had a mighty long haul every morning at seven, moving their wares from the vans to the market, then setting up those attention-getting displays. Marlene concluded that she and Kate absolutely had to have an indoor location.

Trekking through the air-conditioned tents, Kate had worried about profit versus operating costs, while Marlene shopped. How would Marlene's "junk" or even her "treasures" generate enough income to defray the rent on an inside table/booth? These out-of-the-sunshine vendors sold upscale items: fine jewelry, cashmere sweaters—oddly enough, very popular in South

Florida—and designer shoes and handbags. Or damn fine imitations.

Now, feeling hot and sticky in the middle of the field of dried grass beyond the circus tent as they returned to their nice, cool corridor, Kate wondered what marketing genius—some Cunningham?—had made the decision to hide the leasing/management office in the dreariest section of the flea market.

Most of the vendors here wore weathered, sunburned faces and an air of desperation bordering on defeat. Maybe with good reason. Not a customer in sight.

Vans were lined up behind tables that held cheap trinkets, haphazardly displayed. The merchandise made both Marlene's "junk" and "treasures" seem like jewels from Tiffany.

Did these vendors sleep in the vans or did they pack up their goods every evening, drive off, and return the next morning? Spotting a clothesline strung between two rear windows, Kate realized for most of the vendors, their vans also served as their homes.

Sean had removed his oversized shoes and was carrying them in his left hand. His right hand clutched Marlene's elbow. Though walking in socks that must be as smelly as they were soiled, Sean still smiled and joked, keeping up a line of clown patter, as if he were center ring.

"Pick up some speed, girls," Sean said. "We're running late for cocktails, and I have another show to do tonight." Squeezing Marlene's arm, he winked at Kate. "Like the lovely Donnie's coddled elephants, don't I deserve to be fed and watered?"

Kate couldn't remember when she'd ever taken such a strong disliking to any human being. His only redeemable trait had been securing them a place in the busy, well-located corridor. But even that beau geste shouldn't be enough to subject her to the clown's ongoing prattle and those disgusting feet.

She'd bet Sean *never* showered and changed between shows. He probably just had a couple of drinks, grabbed a hot dog, reapplied that garish makeup, and then crawled right back into his VW Bug.

Four

The doll lady looked like one: Chronologically Correct Barbie. Mid-to-late forties, Barbie's real-time shelf life. Her strapless, cotton-candy-pink satin top and Lycra miniskirt were the exact shade of her thigh-high leather boots.

She whipped her long golden curls around, the ends of her hair sweeping over Marlene's cheek like a blush brush, gave Kate a dirty look, and snarled. "What's wrong with you, Sean? These women are temporary vendors. Two bloody weeks, for God's sake." She spoke with an English accent and a smoker's rasp, and made it sound as if Kate and Marlene were interlopers carrying the plague. "You're breaking your own Cunningham Circus corridor long-term lease rule."

"Bending, my lovely Linda, merely bending the rule for an old friend." Sean gestured to Marlene with one hand while patting Linda's bare shoulder with the other. "Now say hello to Marlene and Kate. I'm confident that you girls are all going to be great friends."

A beautiful big cat appeared at Kate's feet, wrapping a bushy, gorgeous, but shortened, tail around Kate's ankle.

Kate reached down to pet her new friend, but Linda was quicker, snatching the cat up into her arms. "We don't let strangers touch us, do we, Precious?"

Their less-than-welcoming neighbor let Precious go from her shoulder, paw by delicate paw, onto a pink satin pillow on a shelf behind her. The cat curled up next to a Ken doll with a missing head. Linda adjusted her skirt and returned to the task Sean had interrupted, arranging teeny furniture in a doll-size hacienda. As Linda leaned forward to place a miniature Mexican rug in the hacienda's hallway, her bosom spilled over her strapless top.

Precious woke up enough to play with Ken's torso. Kate and Marlene moved on.

"Don't take it personally, gals. Linda Rutledge's been here for years and has trouble coping with changes in the corridor. High and mighty, that one. Claims she's a distant cousin of Princess Diana. And, of course, she and Whitey Ford were very close. Well, until recently." Sean smacked his ruby red lips and laughed. Such an annoying laugh . . . more like a snort. "Linda never reveals her age, only admits to being somewhere between twenty-one and death. Claims that one day her tombstone will read, 'She Reached Death.' And Linda really lost it when Whitey got drunk and blabbed to all the vendors that her and him were the same age: forty-six."

Sean pointed to a table directly across the corridor from Linda's. "Come on, girls, let's say hello to Freddie."

"First editions," a jolly fat man wearing a Stan Lee T-shirt, said. "Mostly Marvel. Welcome to the corridor, ladies." He gestured to the tall metal racks—all holding comic books—that lined the tent wall behind him. "I'm Frederick Ducksworth. Freddie to my friends."

Kate extended her hand. "I'm Kate Kennedy, and this is Marlene Friedman."

She didn't miss the considerably younger comic book vendor's head-to-toe approving appraisal of Marlene. True, with her expensive makeup and two-hundred-dollar-an-ounce perfume, her platinum blonde sister-in-law, a very large woman, exuded an ageless sex appeal. Also true, Marlene looked most attractive today in her red linen shift with a slit exposing one tanned-to-toast leg.

Kate, neat in pressed khakis and a white cotton man-tailored shirt, suddenly felt old, bland, and sexless. Marlene was always after Kate to "stop dressing like a guy." But Charlie had admired what he'd called her Katharine Hepburn style, and she'd never shown much leg, not even when her silver hair had been chestnut and her freckled, pale-turn-red-never-tan skin had been taut.

"So what do you think of my collection?" Freddie nodded, clearly anticipating praise.

"Impressive." Kate spoke the truth and felt some guilt. Her sons, Kevin and Peter, still angry that she'd tossed their comic books during a June Cleaver–like cleaning spree, would want to buy the lot.

"What will you be selling?" Freddie exposed big teeth framed in a wide smile, topped with sharp blue eyes and bushy white hair.

"Fifties and sixties memorabilia. Hula hoops and poodle skirts. Genuine mink false eyelashes and micro-minis." Marlene winked. "And let me warn you, Freddie, I may have a Marvel or two in my collection." Not only had Kate's former sister-in-law defined her junk, she'd flirted with the competition.

Kate glanced across the corridor to the barren table next to the doll lady's. Gesturing, she said, "We'll be setting up shop over there, tomorrow." Good Lord. It felt as if she and Marlene were jumping into Whitey Ford's turf before the body was buried.

"Two nice-looking, refined ladies like you will do just fine," Freddie said, meeting and holding Marlene's eyes. "See you in the morning."

"Freddie and Whitey haven't spoken to each other since the hanging-chads election." Sean's whisper came through a snortlike laugh as they walked away.

At the table next to Freddie's, a mother/daughter team was selling costume jewelry from the forties and fifties. "The finest retro-design originals in South Florida," the sixty-something mother, Suzanna Jordan, gushed. A slim, classic beauty with great cheekbones, she wore what had to be a Brooks Brothers white cotton shirt and man-tailored tan gabardine trousers. Kate smiled, loving the woman's style and suddenly feeling much better about her own outfit. "And this is Olivia, my daughter," Suzanna said with less enthusiasm.

Her plump, dowdy daughter stared down at the ground.

Marlene picked up an amethyst brooch and held it up close to her eyes. "Miriam Haskell?"

"Exactly," Suzanna said. "Do you own a Haskell piece?"

"Oh, yes, indeed I do. At least twenty, I'd say, not counting the earrings." Marlene smiled. "I may be selling a few of them, myself."

Suzanna did not seem amused.

The trio crisscrossed again, headed to the booth located on the far side of the doll lady's.

"Olivia had the hots—er—a crush on Whitey, but her mother put the kibosh on that." Sean said.

Was the clown a harmless gossip or a born trouble-maker? Kate leaned toward the latter.

Kate gasped, her breath seeping out slowly like a muted shocked whistle. German helmets, Iron Crosses, and an SS black leather trench coat were among the WW II Nazi memorabilia spread across a swastika tablecloth. Hanging on the tent's canvas fabric behind the table were two large U.S.A. wartime posters she remembered from her early childhood. "Loose Lips Sink Ships" and "Uncle Sam Needs You." Part of a recruitment campaign.

The juxtaposition of Nazi Germany's mementos and

WW II America's patriotic slogans disturbed her, rattled her.

The soldier-straight senior citizen, dressed in head-to-toe black, offered his hand. "I'm Carl Krieg." He bowed, merely a brief bob of chin toward chest, but with his graying blond hair slicked straight back, comb lines showing, the tall, thin man's demeanor somehow reminded Kate that Hitler's Youth had grown old. "Welcome to the corridor."

As she'd expected, he pronounced it *velcome.*

"Frau Friedman, isn't it?" The vendor smiled at Marlene.

Good Lord, not another of Marlene's former dance partners from Ireland's Inn. Kate shuddered. Not possible. Marlene wouldn't . . .

"Kate, Mr. Krieg has made an offer on one of those newly renovated condos on the top floor."

"Have I passed muster?" The vendor sounded eager.

"We're still reviewing your application." Marlene sounded icy cold.

Her former sister-in-law served as president of the Ocean Vista board of directors. Eleven years ago, Marlene had purchased a first-floor unit with a balcony only a couple of feet above the sand. Kate had a third-floor unit, also with an ocean view. She and Charlie had moved to Palmetto Beach last April because he'd fallen in love with Ocean Vista during their many respites from cold New York City Februarys when they visited Marlene.

One of the duties of the condo's president and board

of directors was to interview prospective owners. Kate had never heard of a prospect being turned down; but no board member that she knew of would want a neo-Nazi as a neighbor.

They crossed the aisle yet again and approached the last booth on the other side of the corridor, decorated like a gaudy mini-circus and manned by a Cunningham clown—if Kate recalled correctly, the first one out of the Volkswagen.

Sean draped an arm around Marlene. "Watch out for Carl Krieg. That old guy doesn't play well with others. Why, didn't he lose his temper just last week and threaten to punch poor Whitey Ford? They lived in the same rental complex, you know."

Old guy? Kate figured Carl and Sean were contemporaries.

The clown, Jocko, the youngest Cunningham brother, in costume, looked up and smiled at Kate. One front tooth was blacked out. "Pleased to meet you, I'm sure." He turned to his brother. "A great post-matinee crowd. I think we even outsold the doll lady today. I'm closing up shop. It's almost show time."

Though the air-conditioning wasn't too cool, Kate shivered. Something sleazy about that clown Jocko. Something sleazy about the entire Cunningham operation.

Finally free of Sean, they started back to the parking lot. Kate, exhausted and wanting to get home and walk Ballou, wondered if she could work in the corridor.

"Marlene, do you realize that the only vendor Sean

didn't badmouth was his brother, Jocko? He made it sound as if all the others had grudges against Whitey."

"Right." Marlene nodded. "So do you think Whitey Ford's drowning wasn't an accident?"

Kate shrugged. "I'm guessing Sean believes Ford was murdered, so he kept trying, none too subtly, to convince us that everyone in the corridor—except the Cunninghams—had a motive."

Five

"How could I have known that Carl Krieg was some kind of fascist? Hell, he didn't wear his SS black leather trench coat to the interview in the board room."

Marlene's mantra, chanted all during the ride home, had begun to wear on Kate's nerves. "His references were impeccable: a minister, a former governor, and old Mrs. Wagner on the fourth floor. Even Mary Frances liked him, and she'd vet the Pope."

"I only asked about Krieg's application process and its status." Kate sighed. "I'm not accusing you of dereliction of duty." Aware that condo candidates were usually automatically approved, but unable to resist, she added, "You must have noticed his accent."

"What's really going on here, Kate?"

Marlene whipped into her coveted covered parking spot in the owners' lot to the right of the condominium, then stepped on the brake so heavily that Kate was thrown forward. If her seat belt hadn't been fastened, she'd have hit the dashboard.

"Are you mad at me about Carl Krieg's Ocean Vista interviewing process or are you mad at yourself for promising to help me out at the flea market?"

Yet again, Marlene had sliced through the surface muck and gotten down to the swamp at the bottom of Kate's mind where the real problem—the flea market—festered. Kate remained surprised by Marlene's mind-reading skill, though she'd been doing it for decades.

"Well," Kate allowed a small smile. "Maybe the flea market isn't my cup of tea."

"Too Earl Grey or too Apple Spice?"

"Just not Lipton." Kate laughed, acknowledging she seldom varied her routine.

"You're in a rut, Kate. You need to get out of your apartment, meet new people, take a break from sand and surf, our fellow condo owners, and your crossword puzzles." Marlene popped open her seat belt. "I grant you the flea market's not Lord and Taylor's, but branch out, woman. Expand your horizons. Try another brand of tea. Work with me and make some money. Listen, with any luck, Whitey Ford's *accidental* death will turn out to be murder, and you can question the suspects between sales."

They entered by the side door. Ocean Vista's seafoam lobby, furnished with small clusters of rattan tables and chairs, two large dark green chenille couches, and scattered tall baskets holding plastic plants, had faux marble floors and too many mirrors for its aging population. In the center, a life-sized, imitation alabaster statue of Aphrodite stood in a fountain, surrounded by six winged cupids—mixing, probably unintentionally, Greek and Roman myths.

Large even by Florida standards, the lobby boasted elaborate, glass double doors opening onto a circular driveway, edged with royal palms and sweet-smelling jasmine, which swept down to A1A, known in Palmetto Beach as Ocean Boulevard. The rear door led to the recreation room, the pool area, and the Atlantic Ocean.

Though Kate had begun to think of the over-decorated apartment building as home, she still missed the staid red-brick Tudor in Rockville Centre, her real home, where she and Charlie had lived more than forty years prior to moving down here. Charlie, who'd so wanted to live on the beach, had died without sleeping even one night in his dream house.

"Yoo-hoo!" She didn't have to turn around; she'd recognize Mary Frances Costello's bird call anywhere. The dancing ex-nun was vice president of the condo board and, since she'd been principal of a grade school, she sometimes tended to treat her co-owners as naughty children. A glamorous red-headed paradox, Mary Frances, Broward County's reigning tango champion, had turned her only bedroom into a dance studio, complete with barres, wall-to-wall mirrors, and rack upon rack of exotic tango costumes. Her living room housed a huge doll collection displayed behind glass doors in floor-to-ceiling bookcases—ranging from Barbie and Ken to Henry VIII and his six wives.

Boy, did Kate have a new friend for Mary Frances.

"Hi, Mary Frances," Kate said, and kept moving.

"Where have you girls been all day?" Mary Frances's green eyes sparkled like Scarlett's at Twelve Oaks while tempting the Tarlington twins. "I have such exciting news."

Her charm was wasted on Kate. "Ballou's been home alone all day, Mary Frances, I have to take him for a walk. Now."

"I certainly understand the needs of a neglected animal, Kate."

"For God's sake, Ballou isn't neglected," Marlene snapped, her face flaming red.

"Of course not," Mary Frances said. "Don't I know he's the luckiest Westie in South Florida? I've just returned from my first day of training to become a volunteer at the Broward County Humane Society. I'll be working in adoption, placing pets. I just can't get all those poor abandoned puppies and kittens off my mind."

Strange. Ballou, who loved most everyone, barely tolerated Mary Frances. Yet . . . the former nun's volunteer work with the Humane Society impressed her . . . it was more than Kate had ever done.

"If I don't get upstairs and walk my dog, you'll be reporting me for cruelty to animals." Seeing the crestfallen look on Mary Frances's face, Kate relented. "Want to join us?"

She heard Marlene groan.

"You're coming, too, right, Marlene?" Kate was enjoying herself. Marlene and Mary Frances were always sniping at each other. "Ballou would love to see his favorite aunt. And Mary Frances can tell us all about her new job, and you can tell her all about us becoming vendors at the Palmetto Beach Flea Market."

"Talking about cruelty to animals," Mary Frances said, "did you know the Humane Society sent an investigator out there to the Cunningham Circus? Some young elephant trainer supposedly abused an elephant."

"Just give me a minute to change my shoes," Marlene said. "I'd love to go for a walk with you and hear all about it."

Six

"Down, boy," Kate ordered, but it sounded a lot like "I love you." Ballou jumped, yelped, licked, and nipped at her ankles all at the same time, expressing boundless joy at seeing his mistress. Then, to her delight, he held up his right paw as if waiting for a high five. Kate obliged. The high-five greeting had become a ritual between the Westie and Charlie. Kate felt honored to carry on the tradition.

She kicked off her good beige sandals and slipped into her old canvas boat shoes. No time to change her clothes: This dog had to go for his walk.

Ballou, as usual, squirmed and fussed as she struggled to put on his leash. "Stop that! Auntie Marlene and Mary Frances are waiting for us." He cocked his head, staring up at her with soulful eyes, then went back to nipping at her hands. She shook her head and resumed her struggle, knowing he wouldn't calm down till the leash was on.

Obeying house rules, Kate carried Ballou into the elevator and across the lobby, under the watchful eyes of Miss Mitford, keeper of the keys and longtime sentinel at the front desk. A dour woman who'd been at Ocean Vista since the ribbon had been cut on the condominium in the mid-seventies, Miss Mitford ran the desk like a Marine drill sergeant, never allowing any leeway to those entrusted to her care.

Kate pushed open the back door and a cool ocean breeze ruffled her short hair, making her smile. So it wasn't April in Paris—April in Palmetto Beach wasn't bad, either. The sun hovered over the horizon, the sky a pastel palette ranging from soft violet to muted coral. A broad expanse of sand almost devoid of humans led down to the deep blue sea topped with whitecaps that shimmered like whipped cream.

"Wait up!" Marlene shouted the exact same words she'd used over sixty years ago to stop Kate in her tracks; they worked just as well this evening.

Kate spun around, still smiling, in a far better frame of mind than during the car ride home from the flea market. The salt air? Or the anticipation of Mary Frances providing her with a raison d'être? A cause she could champion. Kate liked causes. Missed not having one. Why couldn't she volunteer at the Humane Society, too? Maybe track down the elephant abuser.

"Hi, Marlene." Ballou strained on his leash, pulling

Kate back toward Marlene. The Westie liked most people, but he so adored Marlene that, before Kate and Ballou grew so close, she'd felt jealous of her former sister-in-law.

"Where's Mary Frances?" Marlene had changed into a gauzy aqua caftan and low-heeled sandals, and she'd wrapped an aqua turban around her platinum French twist.

"Right here." The dancing ex-nun rose gracefully from a chair by the pool, barefoot and beautiful. Her red hair glinted in the waning sunlight, and her green sweatsuit matched those sparkling eyes. Only Mary Frances could make sweats look like haute couture.

Ballou, not impressed, growled softly and pulled back when Mary Frances reached out to pet him.

"Your dog doesn't like me, Kate." Mary Frances sounded hurt and indignant. She'd remarked on Ballou's unfriendly responses to her overtures many times before this snub.

"Oh, he only has eyes for his Auntie Marlene." Kate said, handing Marlene his leash. "He even ignores me when she's around." She had a quick word with God, willing Marlene not to comment.

Seeming to get the message, Marlene remained silent, letting Ballou prance like a king several paces ahead of his ladies-in-waiting.

"The staff at the Humane Society has been lobbying the Palmetto Beach Police Department to investigate rumored abuse for some time." Mary Frances, over her snit and aware that she had an avid audience, spoke with a sense of breathless drama. "So far the police haven't done a thing, but after a recent phone call, a volunteer from the shelter visited the circus again and nosed around. She reported that Edgar had suspicious injuries." Mary Frances sounded like a commentator on Court TV.

"Edgar?" Marlene started when Ballou, who'd been chasing a sea gull, stopped short after discovering the bird could fly faster than he could run.

"The elephant. Edgar," Mary Frances said. "He has a sister, Edna. They're named after Poe and Ferber." She shrugged. "Apparently, the trainer has a literary streak as well as a mean streak."

Mary Frances had spoken Kate's exact thought.

"Who called to report the abuse?" Kate kicked a ragged piece of colored glass out of her sandy path, glad she'd worn her boat shoes. The barefoot ex-nun might wind up with some serious nicks on her soles.

"Well, that remains a mystery," Mary Frances said. "He wouldn't give his name, but promised to phone the next day. The director never heard from him."

"Did the caller name the elephant trainer as the abuser?" Kate, rather uncharitably, believed Donna Viera might be capable of behaving that cruelly.

Mary Frances shook her head.

"So, there's no proof. They never heard from him again." Marlene raced ahead to keep up with Ballou but shouted over her shoulder. "Exactly what type of abuse had this guy reported?" She sounded like Court TV, too. The hard-nosed prosecutor.

"Ah, but there is proof." Mary Frances pulled out a surprise, defending the informer. "Yesterday, a package arrived at the shelter. Color photographs showing welts on Edgar's hind legs. Big, ugly welts. It looked as if someone had whipped the poor animal. Hard."

"How do you know those photos were of Edgar? Maybe they weren't even taken at the flea market." Marlene had slowed her pace to stay in the conversation. Ballou circled ahead, waiting for them.

"The elephant was standing under the Cunningham Circus big top." For Mary Frances, case closed.

With Ballou fed and ready for bed, but in no mood to leave the party, the three women sat on Kate's balcony watching the truly glorious sunset with the Westie curled up into a white furry ball at Marlene's feet.

Marlene had mixed a batch of martinis for herself. Kate and Mary Frances sipped white wine. They'd ordered pizza, and Kate had defrosted a homemade apple pie for dessert. Fat city, tonight. She didn't care; she craved comfort food. She couldn't stop thinking about Edgar.

Spearing an olive, Marlene said, "We met that Carl Krieg at the flea market this afternoon, Mary Frances. Turns out he'll be our neighbor in the corridor as well as here in the condo."

"Really?" Mary Frances pushed a red curl away from her left eye. "I've been having some serious second thoughts about that man."

Kate, not missing Marlene's grimace, bit her tongue.

"Why?" Marlene pointed her plastic stirrer at Mary Frances. A gin-soaked olive, the exact color of Sean Cunningham's shifty eyes, dangled from its end.

"I think Krieg might be some sort of neo-Nazi. When I went up to change for our walk, I saw him being interviewed on the six o'clock news. He was wearing a T-shirt with a huge swastika."

"On the news? What were they asking him?" Kate's entire body tingled with the familiar electric charge that heralded fear, excitement, or intrigue. The spark felt good.

Mary Frances snatched the olive off Marlene's stirrer and popped it in her mouth. "About some guy in his apartment house—looked like a rundown rental to me, and I wondered how Krieg could have afforded the down payment on a condo here—anyway, earlier this week, some neighbor, with a name like a famous baseball player, had drowned in his bathtub, under what the police are now calling 'suspicious circumstances.' "

Seven

Murder had moved Whitey Ford from his burial on the bottom of the fourth page to above the fold on the first. Those "suspicious circumstances" that Mary Frances had heard reported on the TV newscast last evening had morphed into a full-blown homicide investigation in this morning's *Sun-Sentinel*.

Kate gulped her too-hot tea, almost without noticing,

too immersed in the story to worry about a slightly singed tongue. The early-morning sun flooded her balcony, so bright she could read without her glasses. Well, the headlines, anyway.

Ballou rested his head on her bare feet, and she slipped him a very small piece of whole wheat toast topped with strawberry jam. "Don't tell Auntie Marlene or she'll have you as fat as a house in no time." Though Kate had strict rules about not feeding Ballou table food, she violated them often. She just didn't want anyone else to find out.

She and Ballou had a busy day ahead of them. Late last night Kate had told Marlene that if the doll lady, Linda, could bring her cat to work, they could bring Ballou. Not only was the Westie well behaved, but Kate would feel a lot better about being at the flea market with her pet at her side. And, in addition to her spirits being lifted, she'd have no guilt about leaving him home alone.

Marlene had smiled, saying, "Of course Ballou's coming with us. He's family."

Much to Kate's surprise, Mary Frances had jumped in. "I have no plans for tomorrow morning. Why don't I help you move your stuff?"

Kate glanced at her watch. Seven-ten. She'd better get a wiggle on. They were meeting at Marlene's apartment in twenty minutes. She stood, still reading the story about Whitey Ford. The police, as usual in these cases, had said little, but Homicide Detective Nick Carbone, from the Palmetto Beach Police Department, had been quoted: "Whitey Ford had company while he bathed."

She smiled as she folded the paper and picked up her breakfast tray. "You know, Ballou, after we get Auntie Marlene's booth set up, I may just have to give my friend, Nick Carbone, a call."

Ballou cocked his head, all ears.

Kate laughed. What was she thinking? Nick Carbone might be more than an acquaintance, but he was less than a friend. As with so many things about the man, her relationship to him seemed to defy description. Well, hell's bells, she loved a mystery and, moreover, she had an idea about Whitey Ford—or at least a glimmer of one. She'd give Nick a call regardless of what their relationship was or wasn't. It wouldn't be the first murder investigation she'd horned in on.

The flea market suddenly seemed much more appealing. No doubt there'd be several motives for Whitey's murder right under her nose in the corridor. Not to mention clues. She'd ask a few questions, no harm in that.

She'd tossed and turned most of the night, dreaming about taking her boys to the circus at Madison Square Garden, and about how much they'd loved the movie *Dumbo*, and about those cute dancing elephants yesterday afternoon.

As she closed the patio door with one hand, juggling the tray with the other, Kate thought of several questions for Donna Viera.

● ● ●

Chaos greeted her. Marlene's condo, cluttered at best, startled, no, scared Kate. "What happened here?" She edged around an open cardboard box with streamers of silver tinsel spilling over its sides.

"Seller's remorse." Mary Frances popped up from behind a steamer trunk. "Marlene's rethinking what she can part with and what she should keep. No contest. Almost nothing goes."

Marlene headed toward the kitchen, carrying a pile of Tupperware bowls. Glancing over her shoulder, she gave Kate a defiant look.

Ballou's ears drooped. His eyes looked out sadly from the thick fur almost covering them. This had to be the first time ever his Auntie Marlene hadn't said hello and made a fuss over him.

Seeing weeks of hard work and harder decisions coming to naught, Kate stifled a scream and said, "Come on, Marlene, you can do this."

Straight ahead, Kate spotted all the hula hoops that had been packed and ready to roll, back out on the balcony. The neat-freak side of her personality kicked in.

"Stop this nonsense. You're hurting Ballou's feelings. And wasting everyone's time. This is unacceptable behavior. Now put those ugly bowls back in the box. We have a place in the corridor leased and paid for and, by heaven, we're going to work."

Ninety minutes later, they made their first sale.

Kate stared at their first customer, wondering could she

have ever been that young? She'd certainly never been as thin or as pretty.

"I must have that brooch. Big pins are in again, and I love retro, don't you?" The blonde girl had her own credit card neatly placed in a Coach billfold that she'd retrieved from a large Coach tote laden with her other purchases. Busy bee, this one. The flea market had only opened an hour ago. Kate figured if the young woman had her own American Express account, either she was eighteen or had very indulgent parents. Probably the latter. South Florida seemed to be infested with spoiled teenagers.

"It's not a Haskell, you know," Marlene said.

The blonde looked blank. Ballou sniffed her feet.

"Cute dog, but I prefer poodles." Kate bit her tongue. No matter how tempted, a saleslady can't lash out at a customer.

Ballou loved being at the flea market. Ears perked and nose twitching, he'd explored shamelessly all the way from the parking lot to the corridor. So many new sights, so many people, so many smells. Kate had kept an eye out to make sure Ballou wouldn't decide a certain smell needed to be marked in his own special way, with a jaunty lifted leg.

The poodle-preferring girl held the pin up to her shoulder. "It'll go great on black satin."

The glass imitation-ruby brooch was so fifties and so matronly that Kate couldn't imagine Marlene ever wearing it, though they'd all worn fat flowerlike lapel pins back then. More puzzling was why this trendy

44

teenager, with her bare midriff and white shorts that clung to her fanny, would be interested in this quaint piece of costume jewelry.

They were still unpacking. Mary Frances had tackled the box marked jewelry and arranged all the earrings, pins, and bracelets in the plastic display trays Kate had bought at the Dollar Store. Nothing had been priced. And Kate couldn't remember where she'd stuck the tags.

"How much?" The girl fingered the brooch. "I can't live without it."

Marlene slowly turned from Kate to Mary Frances. Kate held her breath.

"Two hundred and fifty." Marlene sounded firm.

"Great." The girl grinned. "Do you have earrings to match?"

Except for the three of them, giggling guiltily in the wake of their first customer, the corridor was quiet. The vendors here worked a late shift in order to catch both the matinee and the evening crowd.

When Kate had arrived in the corridor at eight-thirty this morning, lugging a big carton, Jocko, who'd been sweeping the floor, dropped his broom and gave her a hand. Thinking Sean must work his relatives round the clock, Kate had nevertheless been grateful for the clown's offer to help. And he'd ordered two of the circus roustabouts to leave their chores and "help the ladies set up shop."

Now at nine, with only half the cartons unpacked,

they'd made a big sale.

"I think this calls for a celebration," she said. "I'll go get some coffee for you two and a cup of tea for me and three of those sinful jelly doughnuts from the bakery in the food tent."

"Make mine strawberry," Marlene said, caressing the AMEX receipt. With the matching earrings, their first sale had totaled three hundred and thirty dollars. Kate's thirty percent came to ninety-nine dollars. She might learn to like this job.

On her way to the food tent, Kate made a detour. Yesterday, she'd passed a booth selling signs and posters, created on the spot in big, bold, black calligraphy. She ordered a large poster, saying "Past Perfect." Marlene once said she liked that name.

"I'll be back in an hour to pick it up, okay?"

She stood in line at the bakery counter, trying to decide if she wanted strawberry or raspberry jelly. Mary Frances had opted for a chocolate doughnut.

A snortlike laugh caught her attention. Right in front of her, Sean Cunningham, as scruffy out of clown costume as in, had his arm around Donna Viera's waist, and his head bent close to the animal trainer's ear. But not so close that Kate couldn't hear him whisper, "You don't tell that Humane Society dame a goddamn thing, you understand me, Donnie?"

Eight

Where the devil was Kate? Ten more minutes of Mary Frances dancing around in cheery collaboration— "Where would you like this, Marlene? . . . Doesn't that Pucci scarf just shout, 'Buy me'?"—and Marlene would have to kill her. Truth be told, she didn't much like Mary Frances, Broward County's tango champion. And she had to put up with the ex-nun—prettier and bossier than Maureen O'Hara in *The Quiet Man*—as vice president on the Ocean Vista's board of directors. Enough already. And what in the world could be taking Kate so bloody long?

"You want I should put this last carton down next to the booth, Miz Friedman?" Jocko juggled the heavy package, a pleasant smile on his round, careworn face. "I don't want to stop your progress. Hard to believe how much you got unpacked in such a short time. The redhead's some organizer, ain't she?"

Mary Frances, overhearing, smiled at Jocko, almost flirting. Then she pointed across the corridor. "That swastika tablecloth must belong to Carl Krieg. Disconcerting isn't it? Marlene, aren't you concerned that all that Nazi memorabilia will repel your prospective customers?"

"That's the least of my worries." Though tempted to tell Jocko to drop the box on Mary Frances's well-shod foot, Marlene smiled. "Please put the carton next to the table. And thank you, you've been wonderful." She

47

pulled three twenties from her purse. "Here, please split this with the other two guys who helped us out." Jocko walked away grinning; she wondered if he'd pocket it all. She sighed, then glanced at her watch. Almost ten. The flea market had managed to turn her into a total cynic in less than an hour.

Her conscience bothered her. A chronic condition. A bit better judgment and fewer lies of omission, and she'd fret a lot less. Hadn't she learned anything from her checkered past? Apparently not. Sometimes, she wished she could pop a Pepcid AC the way Kate did for stomach distress and make her bad memories disappear like a gas bubble.

Ballou jumped up gently, putting his front paws on her knee. Looking wistful, he licked her hand, nibbling it.

"You're such a good boy," Marlene said, feeling better about herself. He seemed to understand and tried to lick her face.

Mary Frances stamped her foot. "Are you day-dreaming? Or going deaf? What about my display? Do you prefer these white leather frames front and center, or shall I move them to the back of the table?"

Marlene shook her head and held her tongue. After all, the woman, annoying as she was, had volunteered her time and—much as Marlene hated to admit it— talent. "No. They look great there. Thanks."

Silence filled the corridor. It occurred to Marlene that, without Kate around, she and Mary Frances had nothing to say to each other. Ballou, who'd never cottoned to Mary Frances, circled a carton, then settled back down at Marlene's feet.

She felt undeserving of the Westie's devotion, even though he'd liked her from the day they'd first met in Kate's kitchen in Rockville Centre. Charlie Kennedy had brought him home as a puppy, a tiny white ball of fur, cute as a teddy bear. Ballou always had been very much Charlie's dog, slow to warm up to Kate, yet perversely fond of Marlene.

All that changed when Charlie dropped dead. Kate, in her grief, and Ballou, deprived of his master's attention, had turned to each other. What had started out as mutual comfort and companionship had blossomed into true love.

But Ballou had love to spare, and he still made a great fuss over his Auntie Marlene.

She sighed, a sharp release of breath, muttered "damnit" under her breath, and drew an odd look from Mary Frances, who was emptying the contents of the last carton.

Marlene went to work, stacking the colorful pottery bowls she'd bought in Arizona almost a half century ago during her brief first marriage. Her hands might be busy, but not as busy as her mind, whirling with images of Charlie.

Why today? She could go for days, even weeks at a time, believing she'd moved on, then unexpectedly, unrelenting panic would grip her like a vise and hold her captive. Betrayal was an ugly act. An ugly word. And Marlene had betrayed Kate.

A four-martini one-night stand with her best friend's husband, during a party that had gone on far too long, on top of a pile of coats in the hosts' bedroom. A fleeting act of adultery decades ago that, though neither had ever spoken of it again, had haunted both their lives. She hoped that wherever Charlie's soul had gone, he'd been forgiven and had finally forgiven himself.

"Marlene, you never mentioned Linda Rutledge has a booth here!" Mary Frances's squeal jarred Marlene. The woman sounded starstruck.

Marlene placed a purple bowl into a larger mustard-yellow one, then looked up. "So?"

Mary Frances ignored her, moving on to greet Baby Boomer Barbie as if she were royalty. "It's such an honor to meet you, Ms. Rutledge. To think your booth is right next to Marlene's. I've tried to speak to you at doll shows, but you're always surrounded by such a huge crowd." Mary Frances was gushing like a fan who'd cornered her favorite rock star. "I'm a collector, too."

Ballou went into alert mode, eyeing a nervous Precious in Linda's arms, signaling with perked ears that he was interested, but wagging his tail just enough to show he wasn't hostile.

"Is that right?" Linda, in purple spandex, placed the cat on her satin pillow on a high shelf, then opened a cabinet door, pulled out a black velvet cloth, and spread it over the table.

Precious stared down at Ballou suspiciously from her safe perch, fluffing her fur and flattening her ears. Her body language said, just let that upstart try to come close, she'd sharpened her claws for just such an occasion.

Ballou showed no fear, going into his treed-a-squirrel pose, waiting. His tail had stopped wagging. That cat wasn't going anywhere without being chased by him. Precious settled into her soft bed, keeping both green eyes on the threat below. Marlene decided their impasse wouldn't soon be broken.

"Oh, yes." Mary Frances said. "I'm one wife short in my Henry VIII set. I heard at the Miami convention that you have a rare Peggy Nisbet gem. Anne of Cleaves. I'd be most interested in getting my hands on Henry's fourth wife."

"Queen Anne is an elusive lady." Linda almost smiled. "I do have her, but as a collector you must realize Henry's wives don't come cheap."

"I'll pay anything." History repeated itself. Mary Frances sounded exactly like the flaky teenager who'd been their first customer.

Ballou wandered off, sniffing his way across the corridor. Good. Marlene didn't want any pet trouble.

She started stacking orange dinner plates, wondering why in the world she'd bought a pottery service for twelve, while listening to Mary Frances negotiate with the doll lady. No question, Linda Rutledge had the upper hand and would get her price . . . which was an astounding six hundred dollars. What kind of a pension did former nuns get, anyway?

Ballou, who'd been sniffing around the swastika

tablecloth, yelped. His barks grew louder and sharper, and he literally ran around in circles.

Marlene dropped a plate as she hustled over to him. "What's wrong, Ballou? Why all the commotion?"

Agitated, the little dog just yelped louder, alternately sticking his nose under the flag and running back toward Marlene.

She reached down to lift the Westie, but he moved too fast. "Stop that! We don't belong here."

Ballou ignored her and using his head, shoved the cloth to one side, revealing a black leather heel.

"Oh, my God!" Marlene screamed, recognizing Carl Krieg's boot and realizing the boot was connected to a leg.

Nine

Donna Viera spun around. Spotting Kate, she sniffed, giving her a long, lingering look that met Kate's eyes and moved all the way down to her feet.

The trainer turned back to Sean, whispering. "The old biddy behind us had an earful."

Sean, slower to note Kate's presence, glanced over his shoulder. "Top of the morning, Mrs. Kennedy."

Not bothering to hide her anger, Kate said, "The old biddy isn't deaf. And, yes, I overheard Sean warning you, Donna, or should I say, threatening you?"

"Now, I didn't mean anything at all, did I?" Sean's rice-pudding face attempted a smile that wound up a grimace. "It's just that those PETA do-gooders sometimes have the wrong idea about what it takes to train an elephant and consider every prod a form of cruelty to animals."

Remembering Donna's forceful prod with the baton, Kate thought the "do-gooders" had the right idea.

"Is there an official investigation, then?" Kate tried to keep her tone flat and neutral, but knew she came off as judgmental.

"No, no. Just some volunteer gal from the Broward County Humane Society who has absolutely no authority to poke." Sean stopped short, looking flustered, as he realized what an unfortunate verb he'd chosen to describe the woman's mission.

Kate decided to pay a visit to the volunteer, but she'd start with the trainer. "Why did the Humane Society believe there might be animal abuse, Donna? Had someone here complained?"

"Those PETA people are fanatics." Donna scowled, almost spitting out her venom. A definite mean streak, Kate thought. "One of those lunatic troublemakers ranted and raved about the tiger's nails being clipped too short." Donna flipped her black ponytail. "I told the old cow she could give Sinbad his next manicure."

"Now, Mrs. Kennedy, there's no reason for you to be fretting over this. The Humane Society dropped the investigation for lack of evidence." Sean spoke with a "been there, done that" attitude. "So, can I buy you a coffee and a muffin?" He'd reached the counter and was gesturing expansively at the array of baked goods.

Lack of evidence, indeed. Mary Frances had mentioned those photographs arriving as promised. Kate would rather dine with the devil himself than have breakfast with Sean and Donna.

"No, thank you. I'm bringing doughnuts back to the booth. We're busy setting up."

"Well, have a good day, Mrs. Kennedy." His smile held no warmth. "And tell my gal, Marlene, that I'll be dropping by later to officially welcome her to the Cunningham corridor."

Donna pointed to a raspberry doughnut and said to the young clerk, "Please give me two of those and two black coffees with extra sugar. Thanks."

After all her rudeness, Donna's good manners when ordering struck Kate as odd.

The flea market was jumping as Kate walked back to the circus corridor, balancing two coffees, a tea, and three doughnuts in a lopsided cardboard carton. She couldn't believe how the crowd had swelled. If she didn't think she'd drop her goodies, she'd glance at her watch. She'd been gone, what, maybe thirty minutes max, and the grounds were packed with people. You couldn't see the grass for the sneakers. Retirees, moms pushing strollers, teenagers playing hooky, and eager young couples, hand-in-hand, buying housewares. Good. Every one of them could be a prospective buyer.

Concern curbed her enthusiasm. Whitey Ford's murder—or, at least, the homicide investigation of his "suspicious death"—and its possible link to animal abuse nagged at her. She didn't want to put a damper on

54

Marlene's debut as a vendor, but she so wanted to talk to the Humane Society's volunteer.

As a toddler on a tricycle bumped into her shins, almost causing the food to fly out of her hands, Kate veered left, and carefully placed her cardboard carton on a wicker chair in front of a booth selling potted palms. She pulled her cell phone out of her pocket. Maybe she'd luck out and the Humane Society volunteer would be on the job.

Early-bird passersby, apparently sated, held shopping bags and totes filled with purchases as they headed back toward the flea market's parking lots. Their replacements, streaming past in the opposite direction, looked eager and determined to find a buy. Kate figured many of them were regulars. If the shoppers didn't go broke, the flea market would be a great place to while away a sunny April morning, enjoying the fresh air and searching for bargains. Far better than sitting at home alone watching sappy talk shows or soap operas.

Kate dialed information, and her tiny cell phone's technology both located the phone number and automatically dialed it for her.

"Broward County Humane Society," a perky voice answered.

"Hello. My name is Kate Kennedy, and I need to speak with one of your volunteers."

"Yes, ma'am. Which one?"

"I'm sorry, I don't know her name." Hell's bells. Why hadn't she thought this through first and asked Mary Frances, who might have known. Hearing a sigh, Kate plunged onward. "I'm looking for the volunteer who visited the Palmetto Beach Flea Market to investigate possible animal abuse."

" 'Mona Lisa, Mona Lisa they have named you,' " the voice sang the first few bars of the famous Nat King Cole song. Smooth and on key.

"I beg your pardon." Kate sounded as puzzled as she felt.

A giggle, then the woman said, "Sorry. I got carried away. I just love that song, and I just love MonaLisa Buccino. Unlike the painting and the song, her first and second names are one name, one word. She's the volunteer you want."

"Oh." Kate laughed. "That's one of my favorite old songs, too. So is MonaLisa Buccino there?

"May I tell her why you want to speak to her?" The perky voice had turned somewhat wary.

"Yes. Please tell Ms. Buccino I may have information that will help her case."

"Good." The voice was friendly again. "MonaLisa's downstairs nursing a sick dog. Give me your phone number, and I'll have her call you. In about an hour, okay?"

Kate left both her numbers and hung up feeling better, yet frustrated. She had so many questions. Impulsively, but from memory, she dialed Nick Carbone's number. Risking being called a busybody Miss Marple—it wouldn't be the first time—she'd share her theory that Whitey Ford was murdered to prevent him from mailing his evidence documenting elephant abuse to

56

the Humane Society. Did his killer know the photographs had arrived?

Nick wasn't there. She left a brief message, then leaned back in the wicker chair, eyes and heart heavy.

"When an elephant squeaks, it means he's happy to see you." A boy about four, certainly no more than five, with golden-brown bangs and huge, dark blue eyes plopped himself down in a child-sized rocking chair next to her. Kate started. The little boy looked exactly like her son Kevin at that age, with the same John-John hairstyle.

She stared at the child, her heart suddenly much lighter. "Is that right?"

"Oh, yes." The boy smiled up at her." "I know all about elephants. Even their secrets."

Kate longed to scoop him up and ruffle his thick hair, but she settled for a smile.

"Please tell me more."

"I sat on a elephant once. I did. And my mommy helped me off." The boy giggled. "I slided down his face. I really did." His navy eyes sparkled. "Right between his big ears."

"What an adventure." This time Kate did reach over to touch his hair. "I once had a little boy who looked just like you."

"Did he die?"

"Oh, no, sweetheart." Kate shook her head. "He just grew up."

"My daddy died."

"Billy, there you are! I warned you not to wander

off." Donna Viera's loud voice made both the boy and Kate jump. "And I warned you about talking to strangers."

"Well, I'm hardly a stranger, Donna."

"You are to Billy. Why, you could be a child abuser. I've taught him not to speak to anyone he doesn't know. That would include you, wouldn't it?"

Donna grabbed the boy's hand and led him away.

Kate bit her lip as the tears fell. How could her pre-conceived ideas about Donna Viera have been so wrong? Despite those drum-majorette looks, she must be considerably older than twenty. She had a son, whose father was dead. The still-vivid image of the trainer prodding the elephant made Kate feel queasy. How did Donna treat her beautiful child?

Ten

Kate walked into a corridor filled with confusion.

Marlene, on her knees, blocked much of what appeared to be a man's body.

Pacing in the center of the corridor, Mary Frances shouted into her cell phone, "Of course, it's an emergency. I wouldn't have called nine-one-one if it weren't."

The Baby Boomer doll lady, Linda Something—Kate couldn't think—was stroking her cat and crying. "Two dead in three days, Precious. It's time to get out of Dodge." A huge sob punctuated her sentence.

Kate dropped the carton, and the three doughnuts

tumbled out as the cups hit the floor, splattering coffee and tea all over her new gray-and-white sneakers.

An agitated Ballou yelped when he spotted his mistress and ran out from under the swastika tablecloth to Kate's side. She bent and scooped him up, pausing amid all the chaos to note how heavy he'd gotten—too many of Marlene's treats.

As Kate murmured, "It's okay," the Westie covered her face in wet kisses.

"Quick, call Nick Carbone, Kate!" Mary Frances screamed. "The nine-one-one operator just put me on hold."

Clutching Ballou, Kate spun around to Marlene.

Her sister-in-law appeared stricken and, despite her tanned face, pale beneath well-applied makeup.

"Is it Carl Krieg?" Kate's voice, barely above a whisper, cracked. She fixated on a black boot. "Is he dead?" Ballou barked, squirming in her arms. "It's okay," Kate said again, thinking it probably wasn't.

"I thought so," Marlene said, breathing hard, as she rose from her knees. "But it seems he's only dead drunk." She lifted a corner of the tablecloth and gestured toward Carl's still, florid face. "Take a whiff. He's passed out cold."

"Why don't you ladies take a coffee break?" Sean Cunningham said. "I'll sober him up. God knows, I've done it often enough, haven't I?" The clown came across as sincere, sounding concerned for all involved.

Where had Sean come from? And how long had he been standing there, observing them?

59

"Give Jocko and me fifteen minutes. You gals go on over to the bakery." He glanced down at the carton and its former contents, then pulled a twenty-dollar bill from his pocket. "My treat."

Both his movements and his dialogue seemed orchestrated.

"Does that invitation include me and Precious?"

Sean crossed the corridor and draped an arm around Linda's shoulder. "Absolutely, my dear." He tucked the twenty into the deep V of her purple spandex T-shirt.

As they sat in the shade of a huge umbrella-topped table near the circus entrance, Mary Frances and Marlene, fighting to hold the floor, recounted what Kate had missed in the corridor while buying the doughnuts.

This time, the doll lady, Linda, had gone for coffee. Since animals weren't allowed in the flea market—except for the Cunningham corridor vendors' special dispensation—Linda had left Precious in Marlene's arms, warning, "Mind you, Mrs. Kennedy, keep your Westie in his proper place."

The Westie in question sat at Kate's feet, watching the cat.

"So, of course, I assumed Carl was dead." Marlene finally finished the story.

"We all did," Mary Frances begrudgingly agreed. "I was terrified, thinking the vendors might be murdered, one by one." She glanced at Marlene.

Kate didn't feel ready to share her brief moment with the beautiful little boy—it had affected her too deeply to be examined just yet. Instead, she launched into her meeting with Sean and Donna in the bakery, and her suspicions that the killer knew Whitey had shot the incriminating photographs.

"A man called the Humane Society." Marlene frowned. "It's a real stretch to conclude that man was Whitey Ford."

"She's right, Kate." Mary Frances again sounded less than eager to be caught agreeing with Marlene.

"Well, we can't prove anything—at least not yet." Kate shrugged. "But I'd bet the condo that Whitey took those photographs and made the call."

"Whitey Ford couldn't take a proper picture to save his arse." Linda Rutledge placed a large cardboard box filled with doughnuts and cinnamon raisin bagels on the table. "The best photographer in the corridor is Freddie Ducksworth."

Interesting, Kate thought, wondering how much the doll lady had overheard. Hadn't Sean whispered that Freddie, the comic-book vendor, and Whitey, the Dewars pitchers vendor, hadn't spoken since the hanging-chad election? Since they were neighbors in the corridor, that must have been awkward, at best.

"I see you kept your dog at bay, Mrs. Kennedy." Linda sat in the empty chair next to Marlene, who stroked a contented Precious, and reached for a bagel. "My favorites. Nothing like them in Liverpool. And I ordered them smeared with cream cheese."

"Ballou is always very well-behaved, Ms. Rutledge." Sitting like a gentleman at Kate's feet, Ballou stirred at the sound of his name and licked her hand, while still watching the cat.

"Call me Linda. And don't bristle. Some mean little dogs thrive on tormenting my poor Precious. And their masters don't give a fig. I meant that as a compliment, Kate. I can call you, Kate, right, seeing as we'll be working side by side." Linda bit into the bagel. "Brilliant."

Kate jumped on the doll lady's attitude adjustment and moved in for the kill. "Of course, please do call me Kate. And I will have a bagel. Cinnamon raisin is my favorite, too. I have one every Sunday morning after church." Out of the corner of her eye, she caught Marlene smirking. Well, Kate might be laying it on thicker than cream cheese, but she told the truth.

The doll lady smiled.

"So, Freddie's good with a camera. Tell me, does he focus on the circus animals? They're such interesting subjects and right under his nose." Kate took a bite of her bagel. "Yummy, aren't they?"

"Righto." Linda swallowed. "Freddie's favorite models are the tigers; he must have five hundred photos of those cats. Always pulling out the latest batch and shoving them under my nose. Freddie believes tigers are brighter than most people and better-looking, too." Linda lifted Precious out of Marlene's lap and rubbed the cat's stomach. "He often reads his comic books to them, claims they can recognize the cartoon characters' names. Drives their tamer wild." Linda shifted Precious to her knees and sipped her coffee. "If you ask me, Freddie Ducksworth is daft."

"What about the elephants?" Kate asked. "Did Freddie ever take pictures of them?"

Linda shook her head, her long hair rolling with the movement. "I never saw him shooting any elephants. Why do you ask?" Kate could almost see Linda's mind working, quickly coming up with an answer to her own question. "Do photographs of the circus elephants have something to do with Whitey's murder?"

The doll lady was no dope. Still . . . could she be playing Kate? Pretending to process new information, while knowing full well the photographs might be a motive? And, maybe, more important, could Linda Rutledge be a woman scorned?

During Sean's steady stream of gossip yesterday afternoon as he'd introduced Kate and Marlene around the corridor, he'd started with Linda's broken romance with Whitey.

Linda met Kate's eyes. "I told you Freddie's a bit off. He's no killer, though. Not bright enough, for openers." She tugged at her purple spandex shirt, trying to stretch the material to cover her cleavage, and she sounded nervous, on edge.

Kate nodded, then kept quiet, hoping Marlene and Mary Frances would do the same.

"I think someone is after us circus-corridor vendors. It began with the automobile crash."

What crash? Where was Linda was going?

"I doubt Carl Krieg had anything to do with that. He

63

just likes dressing up like a storm trooper and strutting about. For him, every day is Halloween. Carl's all style and no substance, just like the Jerry who landed in my aunt Jessica's garden during World War Two." The doll lady sighed. "A pilot, but not a very good one, and not out of his teens. Destroyed my old auntie's tea rose bushes, though he'd been convinced he zeroed in on Ten Downing Street. Kept demanding to meet Churchill."

Again, Kate nodded, leaning in closer to Linda. Mary Frances opened her mouth, and, then catching Kate's disapproving glance, shut it. Precious meowed—a plaintive sound—the cat's tone matching her mistress's.

"Unlike the German's plane, Suzanna's car crash was no accident." Linda shed a tear and let it roll down her face. "Whitey checked it out. Someone had mucked around under the bonnet and tampered with the brand-new Volvo's brakes."

If this was an act, it was quite a performance.

"I'd swear on my auntie's grave, Whitey must have figured out who tampered with the Volvo's brakes. And why everyone in the corridor was in danger." Linda gulped. "And Whitey had a big mouth, especially after a snootful of scotch. Probably told the killer what he knew, signed his own death warrant."

"It's safe to return to work, ladies." Sean's high, lilting voice startled Kate. "We have Carl sleeping it off on a cot in the fire eater's bunk. Suzanna and Freddie are here and open for business. Jocko's manning the fort, watching over both your tables. But customers are champing at the bit, so you'd better hurry back to your posts." He paused, unblinking in the bright sunshine. "Now."

Eleven

Sean Cunningham's imperial attitude grated, but Kate had to admit he'd been right about the customers. She and Marlene, with Mary Frances serving as a most efficient stock girl, had sold almost two hundred dollars worth of those truly ugly bowls, plus a Miriam Haskell pin for another two hundred, within fifteen minutes.

Across the aisle, the Jordan mother and daughter team were doing well, too. Good, Kate thought, not wanting to outshine the competition on their first day. Suzanna Jordan, sleek in all black—ballet slippers, Capri pants, and turtleneck—had been checking out Marlene's wares when Kate, Mary Frances, and Marlene had returned to the corridor. She appeared perturbed when she spotted Marlene's rather large display of Haskell brooches and earrings.

Ballou, admonished to be on his best behavior, reveled in the crowded corridor, greeting each potential customer with friendly, but not overwhelming, curiosity.

At the table next to Suzanna and Olivia, the latter in an unfortunate orange flowered print—and why hadn't Suzanna shared her fashion flair with her daughter?—Freddie Ducksworth's comic-book aficionados, many of them preteens dressed as Spiderman or the Hulk, stood in lines, three deep. The Santa-shaped man, a wide smile fixed in place, obviously thrived on his customers' demands for attention.

The Cunningham Circus booth was closed, and Jocko had disappeared, no doubt changing into his clown costume for the matinee. Of course, that booth made most of its money post-performance.

To their left, Kate and Marlene's neighbor haggled for ten minutes, then closed a sale with a young woman who purchased a bridal doll the size of a well-nourished preschooler for over a hundred dollars a foot.

Precious, curled up in front of a Tudor dollhouse, had slept through the entire transaction.

Only Carl's table, manned pro tem by Sean himself, sold nothing. The pre-circus crowd wasn't into Nazi memorabilia. Or maybe Sean, already in his clown suit and makeup, had turned them off.

Kate handed a florid matron a plastic shopping bag filled with mustard-color luncheon plates, thinking for the twentieth time in as many minutes, there's no accounting for taste. Mary Frances closed an empty carton, glanced at her watch, and stood up. "I'm out of here."

"Can't you stay just a little longer, Mary Frances?" Marlene came across as desperate and close to begging. "You've been such a big help. Say yes, I'll put you on commission."

Yes, Kate would definitely call that begging.

"No, I can't stay. I have an advanced tango class at two. And I need to go home to shower and change. I'm all sweaty." Mary Frances wiped her brow with a paper towel from a roll that Kate, in neat mode, had packed in a carton, along with Kleenex and a small box of antibacterial Wet Ones, confident that all three items would come in handy.

"You're already Broward County's tango champion, for God's sake!" Marlene stamped her foot, causing a sweet-faced shopper to back away from a portable white vinyl phonograph circa 1955. "Why would you want to pay for an advanced lesson?"

Ballou cocked his head and looked intent in response to Marlene's sharp tone.

The dancing ex-nun appeared flustered. "If you must know, I've entered the South Florida Senior Ms. Beauty Pageant, and I need to brush up for the talent segment. One of the contestants used to dance with Donald O'Connor."

Kate's cell phone rang, and she grabbed it, noticing Marlene had been rendered speechless when Mary Frances walked away, giving them a brief wave over one shoulder.

"Kate Kennedy."

"This is MonaLisa Buccino returning your call."

It might be Kate's imagination, but Sean was staring at her, as if straining to eavesdrop. She turned her back on him, facing the shelves on the tent wall. Silly, she thought. Sean would need Superman's ears to overhear her conversation from the far side of the doll lady's booth.

"Thank you for returning my call. I'm working at the

Palmetto Beach Flea Market, and I wanted to discuss the possibility of animal abuse at the Cunningham Circus with you."

"Have you witnessed such abuse, yourself, Ms. Kennedy?"

Kate took a deep breath. Had she? "I may have. Could we meet to discuss this? At your convenience, of course."

"Where do you live?"

"Here in Palmetto Beach. On A-One-A. Near Neptune Boulevard."

"Me, too." MonaLisa had a clear, warm voice. "I live just north of Neptune. I walk my Lab on the beach every evening about six."

"A beautiful yellow Lab?"

"Yes. At least, I think Tippi's beautiful."

"I live just south of Neptune. We've nodded to each other. I'm the woman with the Westie." Kate had stopped—censored—herself from saying *older* woman. Ballou nuzzled her ankle and she bent down to pet him.

"The lady with the short silver hair?" MonaLisa sounded even warmer.

"Right."

"How about us and our dogs meeting near the pier at six?"

"It's a date."

By ten minutes to two, as the last of the stragglers were entering the circus, Kate felt tired, hungry, and exhilarated. They'd had a great time and made a pile of money.

"Can I leave him with you during the performance?" Kate glanced up from sorting silver earrings and saw Donna Viera, in her drum majorette costume, and her little boy, Billy, standing in front of the doll lady's booth. "The sitter didn't show up. Please. I'm totally desperate."

Lots of desperation in the corridor today.

Billy clutched his mother's hand, his eyes downcast, checking out the floor.

"I don't fancy kids." Linda growled. "They don't like me, and I don't like them."

"I'll watch him." The words tumbled out of Kate's mouth with no thought given.

Donna turned from Linda to Kate. She shrugged. "Any port in a storm, I guess." No smile. No warmth. She moved her son in Kate's direction.

Billy's lopsided grin grabbed Kate's heart. "Hi, Billy, we're going to hang out for the next two hours."

His mother took off. No kiss good-bye.

Marlene groaned. Kate knew her former sister-in-law didn't much fancy kids, either. Except for hers and Charlie's.

"It's lunch time. Not a prospect in sight." Kate pointed to the uniformed guard who'd come on duty shortly after their coffee break. "The guard will watch our booth along with all the others. Let's stretch our legs, take Ballou for a walk, and feed this young man."

A happy Billy and an excited Ballou were now nose to nose at her feet.

"Can he be my dog . . . just for today?" The child looked up at her, his big blue eyes dancing.

Joy engulfed Kate, warmth flooded her body. Decades disappeared, youth returned. A little boy needed her again.

Twelve

Kate answered her cell phone with sticky fingers. In the mid-afternoon sunshine, vanilla-fudge ice cream dripped out of the bottom of Billy's waffle cone at an alarmingly fast speed. She'd tried to ebb the flow by shoving a wad of napkins under the leak.

Marlene, who knew better, was sneaking a small piece of chocolate icing from her Dove bar to Ballou.

"Nick Carbone, returning your call. What do you want?" The detective didn't sound happy.

"I'm fine, thank you. And how have you been, Nick?" Either the man had never been taught common courtesy or he deliberately chose rudeness as a way of life. Kate suspected the latter.

She pictured him in his messy office, smoking a smelly cigar. Overweight and overbearing, with Brooklyn smarts and capable of surprising insight.

"Why did you call, Kate, to give me a lecture on manners? To make small talk? You're the one who never returns my phone messages." Some truth in that. Even the thought of a social relationship with Nick made her

70

nervous, unsure of herself. Maybe he had a right to be annoyed. Nonetheless, his arrogance grated. "I'm in the middle of a homicide investigation."

"Exactly. And I have information that might lead you to Whitey Ford's murderer."

"Damn it, Kate. I don't want your help—or need it."

Kate wiped Billy's mouth and fingers, a losing battle. "Lick faster," she told him, trying to whisper.

Carbone laughed. "What did you say? Have you gone—"

Choosing to be rude herself, she interrupted. "Look, Marlene and I took over Whitey's booth at the flea market yesterday, and Sean Cunningham went to great lengths to drop the names of Whitey's corridor colleagues with motives to murder him."

"Is that right, Miss Marple?" His voice dripped with sarcasm thicker than the ice cream melting through Billy's cone.

"There's another motive, one Sean didn't mention."

"Yes?" Cold tone, yet she could hear his curiosity.

"Those photographs. I think Whitey Ford made the phone call and sent the photographs documenting elephant abuse to the Humane Society. And that's probably why he was killed." Even as she spoke, her fellow corridor vendors' possible motives kept crisscrossing her mind.

"Now, you listen to me, Kate. Stop playing detective. This case is more complicated than a poisoning in the vicarage."

"But—" She was talking to air. Carbone had hung up. Pesky man, anyhow.

Ballou pranced ahead of Marlene. Billy, still dripping, scrambled to keep up. The Westie delighted in the flea market's many different smells and the nonstop foot traffic. Plastic shopping bags blowing in the breeze, so many children on spring break, shouting and laughing. So many strangers to sniff.

"Rein him in." Kate said, pressing the red END CALL button.

Not everyone was friendly. Some passersby gave them disapproving looks. They deserved every one. Pets were banned from the flea market, and Kate, always law-abiding, felt guilty about breaking the rules.

"We'd better head back," Marlene said. "I don't like leaving the booth unmanned—unwomaned, I should say."

"The guard's on the Cunningham payroll; he'll protect our stuff."

A huff wrapped itself around Marlene like a blanket, and Kate ceded ground. "You and Ballou go on back. I'll take Billy for a walk, I need to pick up something."

"What?" Even Marlene's voice sounded huffy.

"Never mind, it's a surprise."

"I like surprises," Billy said, glancing shyly at Kate.

"You shall have one." Kate remembered a Bucking Bronco ride near the calligraphy booth. And surely she could find a table selling toys. Maybe a truck. Peter and Kevin had been crazy about toys-on-wheels at Billy's age. Dump trucks and Dino the dinosaur. Kevin could spell *brontosaurus* before his third birthday.

Ballou seemed happy to go off with Auntie Marlene, but Billy was upset that Ballou couldn't come along with him and Kate.

He'd forgotten all about the Westie by the time Kate hoisted him up on the Bucking Bronco. She smiled, full of pride, wishing Billy were her grandson, as he yelled and cheered, bouncing about and tossing up and down on the mechanical horse.

After two turns, Kate convinced him to move on. Excited, Billy chattered away about cowboys and Indians. And horses. Should she rethink that truck?

They entered the arts and crafts tent to a blast of welcome air-conditioning and approached the calligraphy table hand-in-hand.

Kate was admiring the PAST PERFECT sign when she spotted Suzanna Jordan and Freddie Ducksworth in front of a nearby booth containing sympathy cards. Their voices were raised, and they appeared to be quarreling.

"You're insane, Freddie!" The ladylike Suzanna screamed like a banshee.

Shoppers stopped in mid-transaction. The calligrapher dropped the PAST PERFECT sign. A startled Billy clung to Kate, who caught the sign before it hit the ground.

"You degenerate. How dare you suggest my Olivia was romantically involved with Whitey?"

"Photographs don't lie!" Freddie waved a black-and-white glossy under Suzanna's nose. His customer-friendly round face twisted with rage, so red and strained his cheeks looked ready to explode.

Suzanna's slim, black-clad body moved like lightning; she grabbed the photo, crumpled it with one hand, and slapped Freddie hard across the face with the other.

"Haven't you ever heard of negatives?" Nothing funny about the comic-book vendor's delivery of that line. Freddie Ducksworth sounded not daft, but dangerous. "I'm considering giving one to the police."

"You're a lying vulture."

"No, not a vulture. A man with excellent, owl-like night vision. A photographer who aimed his camera through Carl's window at just the right moment. A witness who will testify under oath about everyone who arrived to visit Whitey on the night he enjoyed his last bath."

Thirteen

Except for the guard, the corridor was empty. Marlene and Ballou could have extended their lunch hour, enjoyed themselves. Kate had some secret mission up her sleeve, and Billy was a cute kid, as kids go. Marlene didn't much like being here with neither competitors nor customers.

Sitting alone at the dead man's table, where he'd been a vendor for so long and until so recently, struck her as eerie and wrong, almost like robbing a cemetery. Kate's instinct had been right. They'd metaphorically jumped into Whitey Ford's grave.

Though she always complained about the heat, Marlene started to shiver. Well, hell, she'd better get hold of herself. Sean would have leased Whitey's spot to the first hot prospect. Why shouldn't she have been the one to take advantage of the situation, sad as it was?

Laughter and screams of delight wafted from the circus into the corridor. Soon that happy audience would be turning into potential buyers. The thought cheered her up.

She stood. "Ballou, it's just you and me. Kate's left you for a younger man with big blue eyes."

The Westie nuzzled her ankle and jumped up to lick her hand, almost as if he understood what she'd said. He often seemed to sense or understand more than most animals. She bent and scratched his ears. "Smart boy, aren't you?"

Ballou chewed her hand in agreement.

"Not as smart as my Precious, of course, but for a dog, he's pretty cute." The doll lady had returned from lunch. Linda carried her cat in a purple tote bag that matched her own outfit. Marlene noticed that Precious wore a purple bow on her collar, as well. "We went off campus for lunch. I really like the House of Pancakes. All that free coffee. And Precious just loves their blueberry syrup."

Dog and cat were both on alert, defensive, but Marlene felt glad to see Linda, who put Precious on a high shelf celebrating Mexico. The cat searched for a cozy spot on the geometric tapestry and closed her eyes. Siesta time at the dollhouse hacienda.

"Where's Kate?"

Marlene shrugged. "I don't know. She had an errand, and she wanted to take Billy for a bronco ride."

"Poor little lad." Linda pulled out a mirror and reapplied her lip gloss. "His mum is no better than a trollop, is she?"

Marlene had no strong convictions about Donna's sex life, but she did have concerns about Donna's treatment of the circus animals, so she encouraged Linda to keep talking. "I don't like her much, myself."

"Why would you? That tart has slept her way through South Florida, hasn't she? And there's considerable evidence to back up the theory that Donna did him in. We corridor people all consider her the prime suspect in Whitey's murder."

Marlene felt inexplicable sympathy for Donna. Maybe something to do with Marlene herself, waking up a lifetime ago in a Sarasota hotel room with a midget in her bed.

"What evidence, Linda?" Curiosity about a current murder took precedence over a checkered past.

"Well, Donna took him to court in a paternity suit, didn't she?"

"Good Lord! Is Whitey Ford Billy's father?" Marlene didn't shock easily, but this news staggered her. She grabbed the table for support.

"Not according to the accused, but the judge ordered Whitey to pay child support. DNA doesn't lie, does it?" Linda fussed over a Marilyn Monroe doll, adjusting the teeny high-heeled shoes, then moving her to a more prominent spot at the front of the table. "Circus audiences fancy celebrity dolls. I usually display my Marilyn Monroes next to my Jackie Kennedy bridal dolls. They provide an interesting contrast, and my customers often buy the pair, but I'm clean out of Kennedys."

"Good marketing plan, Linda." A sly twist, Marlene thought, but she couldn't focus on the doll lady's marketing strategies right now, her heart was racing too fast. Billy told Kate his father had died, but who would have guessed he'd been murdered? Talk about twists. "So, tell me, did Whitey pay child support to Donna?"

"At first. But he's not paid her a penny for the last year. Spent most of his money on booze, the ponies, and the ladies. Selfish sod. Not that Donna behaved any better. She was about to haul him back to court. He tried to appease her, saying he'd provided for Billy in his will. They had a big fight right here in the corridor. Donna screamed at Whitey, 'You're only forty-six. Billy and I can't wait for you to die of old age.' Heard her with my own ears, didn't I?"

"Do either of you ladies know where my mother is?" Marlene hadn't seen or heard the Jordan girl approach. She sounded upset. What was her name? Olive? No, Olivia. Such a sackcloth-and-ashes outfit. And an attitude to match. Could the young woman be doing penance? Still, she had great skin and fine features. With the right makeup, Olivia would be very pretty. Why couldn't Mama Suzanna, the svelte fashion plate, have passed down clothes and cosmetic tips to her daughter? Wasn't that what mothers were for?

"Hasn't come back from lunch yet," Linda said, placing an adorable miniature, black patent-leather hatbox next to the Marilyn Monroe doll. "Didn't you eat with Suzanna today?"

Marlene put on her glasses to read the price tag on the hatbox. "Sorry, I haven't seen your mother, either."

Olivia whirled around, checking out the other booths. "Where is everyone?"

"Odd, isn't it?" Linda asked another of her cockney-style questions that required no answer. "The matinee's almost over, the guard's on break, and most of the corridor vendors have gone missing."

A fresh surge of panic jolted Marlene. Could something have happened to Kate and Billy?

"What about Carl Krieg?" Olivia asked. "Has he woken up yet?"

Linda glanced at her Mickey Mouse watch. Freddie Ducksworth had one just like it, Marlene thought as she stroked a restless Ballou, trying to shake off a deepening sense of impending doom.

"No," Linda said. "Carl's been sleeping for over six hours. Any respectable drunk would be back in action by now."

Olivia sighed. "I went home for lunch. Mother had a date with someone, so I drove over to the beach; we live on A-One-A, you know." She spoke quickly, as if she had to get her story out, but enunciated like a prep-school student. "I picked up the mail. I'd ordered a book of poetry from Amazon, and I wanted to see if it had arrived, thought I might start it over lunch."

Was Olivia going anywhere with this tale? Despite her good diction, she'd started to ramble. Marlene pulled a Kate and just nodded. Even the opinionated Linda, who shot a puzzled look at Marlene, was listening for once.

"And there in the mail was a note from Freddie." The young woman sounded sick. "A very cruel note."

Ballou began to bark. Sharp, repetitive barks, demanding Marlene's attention.

He darted over to the circus entrance, getting more and more excited. His sharp barks took on a staccato beat, bordering on hysteria.

"It, it . . . I think Freddie is trying to blackmail us." The girl shuddered. "Blackmail me."

"Shut up, Olivia." Suzanna strode across the corridor, just as Marlene smelled smoke.

Ballou ran back to Marlene, urgency in every movement. He kept up his cadence of barking.

"Smoke!" Linda screamed, pointing to the circus door. "There's a fire in the Big Top!"

Marlene watched as smoke seeped in. It smelled like logs in a damp chimney.

Ballou kept barking out his high-pitched alarm. Marlene shouted, "Good dog!" She grabbed the cash box and the Muriel Haskell display case and followed him toward the tent's exit, yelling, "Everyone, get out, now!"

Fourteen

"Come on, Billy, Marlene must be having a fit." Kate toyed with the idea of calling her sister-in-law, but then she'd have to listen to two lectures: one now, and one when she arrived in the corridor.

They'd settled on a fire truck, complete with all the bells and whistles, including a hook and ladder. Billy's eyes had lit up like a Christmas tree when its siren had gone off. The cowboy on horseback was tossed back onto the toy vendor's table, and Billy couldn't stop talking about his new "fruck." Kate's older son had had the same problem, pronouncing "truck" as "fruck," leading to a very embarrassed Charlie who'd walked his son past a firehouse, only to have Kevin shout, "Look at the fruck in garage."

Strolling in the sunshine, holding Billy's hand, Kate felt happier at this moment than any time since Charlie's death.

If not perfect, her marriage had been damn good. Kate would have given it an A most days and an A-plus on weekends.

She and Charlie had married before she could vote. They'd celebrated her twenty-first birthday at Tavern on the Green, followed by a hansom cab ride around Central Park. Charlie, on a patrolman's salary, had scrimped for months, eating tuna sandwiches for lunch and resoling his old shoes.

Though Kate had been a stewardess before her wedding, she'd quit her job because even single women who flew from city to city, offering "coffee, tea, or cocktails" to male passengers, were suspect. A best-selling book spoofing stewardesses, *Coffee, Tea, or Me*, had been taken literally by many men back in those dark ages of crinolines and corsets.

Most married women cleaned, cooked, and ironed, and the only men they served were their husbands.

Kate loved Charlie and, to her surprise, loved being what the *Ladies Home Journal* called a "homemaker."

She got pregnant on her honeymoon and produced Irish twins, Kevin and Peter, eleven months apart. The boys and Charlie delighted her. And that delight proved reciprocal, even contagious. Her beloved brick Tudor in Rockville Centre housed four very happy people. If outsiders saw her as *only* a wife and mother, she considered it high praise: The tough homicide detective had treated her like a partner, and he'd turned out to be a great dad and an even greater husband.

"Oh, Charlie, I miss you."

"Who are you talking to, Mrs. K?" She'd asked Billy to call her that, wishing she could have said, "Call me, Nana."

The boy sounded worried. Oh, God, she didn't want him to think his temporary sitter was a fruit loop.

"No one, dear, just thinking out loud."

Billy gazed up at her through his thick lashes. ""No one ever says 'dear' to me. I like it, but I'm Billy. William Robert Ford. Mommy says my daddy died."

Kate swallowed a gasp. She had to seem as if she

were just making conversation and avoid any probing that might upset him. "I'm sorry, Billy. You must miss your father."

The boy clutched the fire truck to his chest as if he expected someone to snatch it away.

"My daddy was a busy man. My mommy said so."

"You didn't spend much time with him?"

"No." Billy sneezed, then pointed to the Big Top. "Look, Mrs. K, smoke! It's good I have my fire fruck."

Kate gaped at the billowing smoke, suppressed a scream, and dialed 911.

"Billy," she said, trying to sound calm, "we need to get help. Let's sit down here." She gestured toward a patch of grass to their right, then turned her back, spoke to the 911 operator, and discovered that she was the fourth person to report the fire.

The wide-eyed boy sat, then reached up and grabbed her free hand.

She wanted to run around the Big Top to the corridor entrance and find Marlene and Ballou, but she couldn't leave Billy alone, and she couldn't put him in harm's way. Frustrated, bordering on panic, she sank to her knees, still holding his hand.

Off in the distance, Kate heard a bell ringing. She pointed to the flea market's main entrance. "Over there, Billy, here comes a real fire engine."

Did she sound as terrified as she felt?

Billy, enthralled by the clang of the fire engine's bell, didn't seem to share her fear. He waved at the fire-fighters as they sped by. A handsome, dark-haired young man tipped his hat and waved back.

The Big Top, small for a circus site but still an enormous labyrinth of a tent, with sections for animals, dressing rooms, and food stands, had three ways to get in and out: A main entrance with a large, well-staffed booth where all tickets were sold in advance and long lines of people waited in the hot midday sun. A corridor entrance where prospective audience members, holding tickets, became customers, shopping in air-conditioned comfort while waiting to see the "second-greatest show on earth." The corridor entrance, a wide double door, had a Cunningham clown, perched on a stool behind a podium, collecting the pre-sold tickets. Its double door always remained closed during performances. The third entrance/exit on the northwest side of the Big Top featured a heavy, roll-up tent door, not unlike an oversized garage door, where the animals and equipment could be moved in and out as needed. Would that exit turn into bedlam as the animals tried to escape?

The main entrance was less than a yard away. Kate recalled her tour with Sean yesterday, when he'd gone on and on about the wonderful traffic control. For the sake of the audience, the employees, and the animals, she hoped Sean's flow plan would work as well as his mouth, but she worried about them all being trampled in a mass stampede.

She watched, in horror, as people started running out and the first of the firefighters went running in. Even with their terrified screams and panicked pushing, the crowd, sharing a common purpose, seemed almost orderly. A burly young man scooped up a frail old lady and carried her to a shady spot under a palm tree.

A second fire truck roared by.

"Is my mommy in there?" Billy, visibly shaken, spoke through tears.

Kate strained, trying to recall a five-year-old child's level of comprehension. "If she is, Billy, the firefighters will get her out."

She pulled the boy close, hugged him hard, and prayed.

Fifteen

Strange, with all that black smoke still spiraling from the tent, there wasn't a flame in sight.

Kate was alternating between frantically dialing Marlene's cell phone—with no answer—and scrutinizing the Big Top, expecting to see the tent go up in a blaze. At least the survivors, though coughing and frightened, seemed uninjured. Many of them, especially those with children, were heading to their cars in the large northeast lot.

Several of the firefighters who'd dashed into the Big Top so aggressively now exited, looking far less stressed.

What had happened in there? Were Marlene and Ballou safe? Dare she risk taking Billy all the way around the circus tent to the corridor entrance?

He'd been weeping off and on, asking about his mommy, wanting to see her. Kate waited for another few minutes—they ticked by like eternal damnation—then grabbed Billy's hand. "Let's go find your mother."

The light in his eyes assured her she'd made the right decision.

By making a wide circle around the Big Top—a long walk for such a small boy, but Billy scampered to keep up—they made it to the outside corridor door without interference.

A firefighter with an ax in one hand and what appeared to be a bowl in the other came running out of the corridor as they approached. Black smoke had settled like smog, turning the air thick, making it hard to catch a breath.

Marlene sat at the same table where they'd had lunch, cuddling Ballou on her lap. The little dog had her whole hand in his mouth, serving the dual purpose of pacifier for him and comfort for her. Huddled close by, Linda held a terrified Precious, whose head was tucked into the crook of her mistress's arm, and a box of Story Book dolls. A shopping bag overflowing with larger dolls was at Linda's feet.

Kate ran over to them, pulling Billy behind her.

The two old friends embraced, both crying, then laughing. "Thank God," Kate whispered. Her best friend could be trying, but what would life be like without Marlene? And Charlie's beloved Ballou, who was becoming Kate's other best friend?

Billy bent and kissed Ballou who backed off, then squirmed toward the boy in delight, licking Kate's arm while trying to jump off Marlene's lap.

"Can I see my mommy?" The boy sounded anxious. "Is she inside with the elephants?"

While Kate struggled with an answer, she glanced around. Suzanna Jordan and her daughter stood back to back, not touching. Olivia, facing the corridor door, flushed scarlet when a fireman walked by, straining her neck to see what he was carrying. Then she sank to her knees, putting her head in her hands.

Kate wondered about Freddie Ducksworth and Carl Krieg. Were they missing?

And what about Suzanna? Had she returned to the corridor right after her screaming match with Freddie? Hadn't Freddie come back? The circus matinee, filled with kids, would have been ending, if all hell hadn't broken loose. Why would the comic-book vendor have left his booth unattended with all those hot prospects about to descend on him?

And where was Carl? Sean had put him to bed hours ago. Could he have slept through all this? Or been injured?

Before Kate could ask Marlene, another firefighter, this one a young woman, coughing and streaked with dirt, came out, carrying a hose.

"No flames in the animal area, either," she said to the first firefighter, blowing her nose.

"If 'where's there's smoke, there's fire' doesn't always hold true, then what's next?" Marlene asked. "Maybe men do make passes at girls who wear glasses."

Kate smiled at Marlene's marriage of an old adage

and a Dorothy Parker quip, glad to see her sister-in-law's sense of irony intact.

"Come on, Mrs. K, let's find my mommy." Billy tugged on her arm.

"You can't go in there, son," the male firefighter said. "That smoke is dangerous."

"I want to see my mommy. Now." Billy threw himself on the grass, feet flying, kicking the heavy air, causing the smoke to move.

"Is everyone out?" Kate asked the young man.

He didn't meet her eyes. "No, ma'am, not everyone."

The thud in her heart sounded so loud, she wondered why the fireman didn't jump. She'd heard that same thud when Charlie had dropped dead at her side after signing the Ocean Vista condo papers, his gold Mont Blanc pen, which the Homicide squad had given him when he'd retired, gleaming as it fell from his fingers when he crashed facefirst onto the desk.

Who had died? Surely this young African-American's sad expression and warm tone signaled death.

Kate glanced at the child kicking in frustration; he'd lost one of his sneakers. Please, God, not Donna. Not Billy's mother.

"Is it," her words tumbled out in a hoarse whisper, "is it a young woman?" She felt Marlene's arm arc around her shoulders. Then Marlene headed for Billy.

The firefighter shook his head. "We do have a young lady with a broken leg, found her hobbling, leading the elephants out. She inhaled some smoke, but she'll be fine. The ambulance is on its way."

Kate said another silent thank-you.

The female firefighter put down her hose and, wiping soot off her nose, joined them. "I'll tell the little boy his mother's asking for him. He can't go in there, but we'll be bringing her out on a stretcher soon."

"Smoke bombs. The bastards planted smoke bombs all over the animal quarters." Sean Cunningham's booming voice preceded him out of the corridor door. He looked a fright. His dirty clown costume and streaked makeup reeked of smoke. "They all got out, but the big tiger will never be the same. Nothing will ever be the same." Sean turned to the doll lady and sighed. "We have to close the corridor, Linda. Imagine that. Close down the whole damn circus while the fire department and the police muck around and investi-gate."

Sean sat on Marlene's empty chair and tried his cell phone. "I couldn't find Jocko. Where the hell is he?"

Linda patted Sean's arm, sort of cooing at him.

"Some of my animals are tied up. Cops and firemen are holding them on ropes and chains, like they were dogs. The damn Miami Zoo has no room for the ele-phants and wants to know if the tigers' shots are up to date before they'll take them."

"It will work out, Sean." Linda sounded like a nurse reassuring a dying man."

"One of the cops said if they can clear out the smoke, even though the circus is a crime scene, the detective in charge probably would let the animals back in and assign some men to take care of them during the investigation."

Sean should have been glad about the cop's suggestion, but he sounded angry.

Kate figured the Palmetto Beach Police Department would draw straws for that fun duty, feeding and cleaning up after four elephants, three tigers, and God knows how many horses and monkeys. And snakes.

"And Donna's hurt, going off to the hospital. Nobody knows how long. Who'll take care of Billy?" Sean whined. "Look at him down on the ground, throwing a fit. Marlene can't control him. I always knew that kid would turn out to be as crazy as his mother and father."

As another siren grew louder, Kate calmly walked over and knocked the chair out from under Sean.

"Have you gone mad, woman?" Sean picked himself up and glared at her.

"Yes," she snapped. "So why don't you just shut up?" So much for her grandmother image.

A second police car pulled up a few yards away, drowning out Sean's protests.

Kate watched a trimmer, firmer Nick Carbone get out. Humph . . . must be eating fewer Krispy Kreme doughnuts and working out. But Homicide on the scene meant that Donna Viera might not be the only victim.

"Who died?" Kate asked the firefighter, speaking quickly. Once Carbone reached them, she'd be sent packing.

"Some old weirdo wrapped in a swastika." The young man shrugged. "Meaning no disrespect, ma'am."

"Smoke inhalation?" She asked, confident that hadn't been the cause of Carl's death.

"Hell, no, ma'am, this guy took a bullet to the brain."

Sixteen

"You have to do it, Mrs. Kennedy." Donna's voice was hoarse, soot covered her face, and her leg had a painful-looking pretzel-like bend to it. "I don't have any family. There's no one left."

Still shocked by this twist of fate, Kate nodded, "Yes, I will. Try not to worry."

How could she refuse a woman on a stretcher, writhing in pain, on her way to Broward General Hospital, and without a friend or a relative to look after her only child?

"The keys are in my bag." Kate could tell it pained Donna to talk. "It's in my locker. Sean has the combination. Go to my house. Get Billy's clothes and his vitamins. Don't forget his teddy bear. He won't sleep without Teddy."

Kate glanced up from Donna's tears to Marlene's frown. Her sister-in-law thought she was crazy. God knows, she felt crazy. Not to mention frightened, inadequate, and used. What did any of that matter? Billy, clutching his mother's hand and crying softly, needed Kate.

The young fireman nodded at the ambulance driver, then turned to Billy. "You have to let go now, sonny. We're going to put your mom in the ambulance. They'll fix her up good as new at the hospital."

"Giving up the Miss Marple role to play Mary Poppins, Kate?" Nick Carbone, annoying as ever, had emerged from the corridor in time to witness her exchange with Donna.

Torn between a sharp retort and a desire to spare the child any more distress, she opted for the latter, and smiled. "Billy Ford, this is Detective Nick Carbone."

The little boy held out his hand. "How do you do?"

Kate thought, not for the first time, Billy's mother had taught him basic good manners. More than she could say for Nick's mother. Though the poor woman had probably tried and given up.

Today Kate had no time for the detective. Motives, means, and opportunity danced through her head, vying for her attention, as mental lists of all the things that she needed to make Billy feel at home at Ocean Vista kept cutting in.

She couldn't wait to sit down with Marlene—the artistic one—and create a flowchart tracking where everyone—especially, the missing Freddie Ducksworth and Jocko Cunningham—had been during the narrow window of opportunity when the smoke bombs had been scattered around the animal quarters.

"I'd like to leave now, Nick, but I need to get Donna's bag from her locker." Kate forced herself to sound pleasant. "Is that okay?"

An hour later, Marlene, Kate, and Billy were in his red, white, and blue bedroom, packing his favorite things.

Next stop, the kitchen to bag his favorite snacks. Double Oreos and Animal Crackers. It came as no surprise that he liked the elephants best.

Billy had been brave all the way to Coral Springs but he'd cried when they had to leave Ballou in the car: no dogs allowed in the animal trainer's building. Now in the Vieras' third-floor walk-up apartment, located in a modest section of the mostly upscale town, the familiar surroundings seemed to soothe the boy.

The small living room smelled of floor polish and lemon-scented Pledge, and the bathroom and kitchen sparkled. Donna slept on a pull-out couch, and Billy had the only bedroom.

"And we have to bring my sheets, the ones with the sailboats."

"How about we bring the pillowcases? You'll be sleeping in my guest room in a full-size bed tonight." Kate gestured to the bunk beds. "Those sheets will be too small."

"What's a guest room?" Billy put his hands on his hips. "I want my own room and my own sheets, or I'm not going. I don't want to sleep in any guest room."

"We'll pack the sailboat sheets, Billy." Marlene started to strip the bottom bed. "And deal with the logistics later."

He smiled—his first since he'd heard his mother was going to the hospital—and ran over to a red toy box. "I have logs. Let's take them, too. I can build a cabin." Bending halfway into the box, he pulled out a plastic container filled with wooden logs. "You can sleep in it,

Marlene." Billy paused, checking her over from head to toe. "It's okay. I'll build a very big cabin."

Marlene roared, her laughter bonding the three of them, making their mission a little lighter.

While Billy and Marlene raided the kitchen cupboards for Billy's favorite foods, Kate, feeling surprisingly little guilt—though her attitude toward Donna had softened somewhat—put on her glasses and rummaged through the maple desk in the living room.

Kate found it odd there was no computer on the desktop, which held several inexpensively framed baby pictures of Billy and one of Donna with a fair-haired, middle-aged man. Whitey Ford?

Even behind closed drawers, Donna remained neat and orderly. She filed her bills in two manila folders, marked "paid" and "to be paid," and her outgoing checks were duly recorded in her checkbook with the balance up to date. More than Kate could say about her own bookkeeping.

But no personal correspondence anywhere. No letters. No cards. No invitations. Nothing.

In the lower left drawer, the last one Kate opened, Donna had stashed clippings from magazines and newspapers in a folder. A mixed bag, ranging from recipes to articles on child-rearing to makeup tips.

Kate was about to put the clippings back in the folder when she spotted an article on animal abuse torn from the *New York Times*: an editorial about the living conditions and treatment of circus animals across the United States. Though Kate couldn't picture Donna reading the *Times*, someone had scribbled in the margin, "Find out how much this guy knows."

Kate stuck the clipping back in the folder.

Laughter drifted from the kitchen, Marlene and Billy were discussing the merits of dropping marshmallows into hot chocolate.

A sliver of something shiny in the rattan wastebasket next to the desk caught Kate's eye. Bits of negatives, cut into small pieces, dotted the bottom of the otherwise empty basket. She scooped them up and walked over to the window, checking each in the bright sunlight.

Tempted to take the pieces home and lay out them out on a table like a jigsaw puzzle—certain they'd develop into a negative of an abused elephant—Kate couldn't bring herself to remove what might be evidence in a murder case.

She dropped the pieces back into the wastebasket, wondering if she'd doomed Billy's mother.

Seventeen

An agitated Mary Frances waylaid them in Ocean Vista's lobby. "There's a woman waiting out by the pool, Kate. Said she had a six o'clock appointment with you."

Ballou yapped, not happily, at Mary Frances. Billy petted him, and the Westie quieted down.

Yikes! MonaLisa Buccino. Kate had forgotten all about her date on the beach with the Humane Society volunteer.

"She has this great big Lab with her. You know Miss Mitford would never allow such a huge animal in the lobby." Mary Frances sounded peeved. At Miss Mitford? No, more likely at the dog and her owner. "The dog's name is Tippi, like the actress Tippi Hedren. She—the dog, not the woman—doesn't like me. Growled and growled. The lady seemed embarrassed by Tippi's bad behavior. She struck me as spoiled silly."

"The dog, not the woman, right?" Kate laughed.

So, it wasn't just Ballou who didn't like Mary Frances. The female Lab had reservations about the dancing nun, too. And Labs like everybody!

"I tell you what, if you'll help Marlene upstairs with all this stuff, I'll go talk to MonaLisa."

"Is he staying here?" Mary Frances smiled at Billy, who was dipping his hand in Aphrodite's fountain, then splashing the water. A wary Ballou watched him protectively.

Miss Mitford coughed. A rebuke missed by Billy, who hopped into the fountain and straddled one of the cupids. Mitford's cough segued to a loud, horrified gasp. As keeper of the condo's keys and enforcer of its rules, the desk clerk sounded both frustrated and furious.

"It's a long story," Kate said to Mary Frances, then turned her attention to Billy. "Get out of there right this minute, young man, and take off those wet shoes." Whirling back to Mary Frances, she added, "Marlene will fill you in while you two unpack. Then maybe we all can have dinner together and celebrate Billy's arrival. My treat." She hoped Marlene had packed an extra pair of sneakers for her guest.

The Humane Society operator had burst into song to describe MonaLisa Buccino, and now Kate understood why. The woman's classic beauty reminded Kate more of Nat King Cole's song than of Da Vinci's painting.

Words and music rushed through Kate's head, transporting her back in time . . . a chestnut-haired girl sitting in front of a grainy black-and-white television set in her mother's neat, floral-print chintz living room, watching *The Hit Parade*'s Snooky Lanson sing "Mona Lisa," the show's number one song for the fortieth straight week.

"Hi, sorry to keep you waiting. I'm Kate."

The yellow Lab, as pretty as her owner, tensed when she saw Ballou. Then Tippi, more than twice the Westie's size, dropped to a submissive position on her stomach, acknowledging the older Alpha dog. Neither of them barked, a hopeful sign. And Tippi, realizing Ballou, wasn't a threat, sat up.

The tall, slim brunette—she looked a lot like Suzanna Jordan—smiled, extended her hand, and said, "And I'm MonaLisa. Nice to finally talk to you, Kate, after all those passing nods. Shall we walk these dogs?"

Both dogs understood the word *walk*. Their tails began to wag in earnest and they sniffed each other.

Dusk often made a dramatic entrance during April in South Florida, preceded by spectacular sunsets and purple-muting-to-violet horizons over the ocean.

At twilight, as Kate and MonaLisa walked north toward the Palmetto Beach pier, the sun seemed to be sliding down behind the blue velvet sea and above them, in the Technicolor sky, a silvery new moon waited in the wings.

Ballou, asserting himself as the only male in the group, led the way, moving at a fast clip, and ignoring Tippi.

MonaLisa made easy conversation, telling Kate all about her duties as a volunteer at the shelter. How she'd be assigned a sick or mistreated stray and would help nurse the dog or cat back to health. And she worked as a nurse—for humans—in her day job.

"Tippi's beautiful." Kate spoke with total honesty. The yellow Lab was a magnificent animal.

"Yes, isn't she? I named her for Tippi Hedren, who's done so much work for animal rights."

Kate, basking in the still-warm rays of the setting sun and savoring the slightly salty air, was jolted back to reality. She had lots of questions on that very subject, and MonaLisa Buccino, no doubt, had some answers.

"Another vendor was murdered at the flea market today," Kate said. "In the animal quarters at the circus, shot through the head." That ought to open up a meaningful dialogue.

"Good lord, not Freddie Ducksworth!" MonaLisa sounded stricken. Not the reaction Kate had expected. "I heard there'd been a fire or a smoke-bomb scare at the Cunningham Circus, but the news didn't mention any murder."

"No. Not Freddie. Carl Krieg. Why did you think Freddie might be the victim?"

"The Nazi? Dreadful man. Still, why him?" Mona-Lisa brushed stray tendrils out of her eyes. A light wind had kicked in, swirling sand around and wreaking havoc on hair. "Carl Krieg lived in Whitey Ford's apartment building, you know, on the first floor, facing the street. I wonder if he saw something or someone on the night Whitey was murdered."

Kate nodded. "Possibly." This afternoon Suzanna Jordan had screamed at Freddie Ducksworth after he'd accused her daughter. Freddie, by his own admission, had been at Carl's apartment that night. If he'd been telling the truth—and he claimed to have the photographs to prove it—Olivia had been at Whitey's, too.

"I'm convinced someone murdered Ford to prevent him from sending those elephant-abuse photographs to me." MonaLisa sighed. "Of course, his killer didn't know he'd already mailed the pictures, so, you see, Whitey died in vain. Somehow, I feel responsible."

"You do? Why?"

"If I hadn't been nosing around, conducting my own unauthorized investigation, Whitey Ford would still be alive." She bit her lip.

Kate sensed that MonaLisa was holding something back. What? And why?

"Tell me, why did you think Freddie Ducksworth had been shot?"

"Because, Kate, Freddie's the one who really took those photographs. Whitey just wanted the glory. Or to impress me. Who knows? But his lie led to his dying. And now Krieg is dead, too."

Her stomach's craving for a Pepcid AC told Kate that MonaLisa was still holding back. Time to push the envelope. "Any idea who killed them?"

Ballou shook his head as a gust of wind blew sand in his face. Tippi pulled her mistress, and veered south, where the wind would be at their backs.

MonaLisa smiled, a slight, enigmatic smile, showing no teeth. "Donna Viera, of course, to protect herself from facing animal abuse charges. Any woman who could mistreat an elephant is capable of murder."

Eighteen

If Kate didn't come back soon, Marlene would have to send Billy to his room and Mary Frances upstairs to her condo.

Two things Marlene long suspected to be true had now become self-evident: A—she'd made the right choice not to reproduce. And, B—despite the ex-nun's sexy, sophisticated façade, inside Mary Frances Costello beat the heart of a silly, self-absorbed teenage girl.

Whine. Whine. Whine. Billy wanted to go to the beach and find Kate and Ballou. Not even building a log cabin to house Marlene appealed to him anymore. He wanted his mother and, if he couldn't have her, he wanted Kate.

What Mary Frances wanted was to bore Marlene and

Billy to death with tales of the Ms. Senior South Florida Pageant, her potential rivals, and the judges' lack of appreciation for the intricacies of her tango routine for the talent competition. Whine. Whine. Whine. Way worse than Billy.

One more word about that bloody pageant and Mary Frances was out of here. As a former teacher, why the hell couldn't she entertain Billy?

"Enough, already." Marlene rose to her feet with purpose. "We're going to surprise Kate and fix dinner. I'm the chef, and you two," she glared at Mary Frances and Billy, who'd shut up and were listening, for a change, "will serve as my sous chefs. Now, both of you go wash your hands, then follow me to the kitchen."

While Mary Frances led Billy to the guest bathroom, Marlene mixed a pitcher of martinis. The first step to a balanced meal. Then she concocted a Shirley Temple for Billy, ginger ale and grenadine, topped off with two maraschino cherries and a straw. For a fleeting moment she considered adding a shot of gin, thinking it might make him sleepy, but settled for a third cherry. Mary Frances could make her own damn drink.

Marlene prided herself on her cooking—innovative, if somewhat sloppy—but after shooting off her big mouth, she wondered if Kate had the makings of a meal in her pristine kitchen. Their tolerance for each other's foibles remained a testament to their friendship.

For sixty years, ever since the first grade, the messy Marlene and the orderly Kate, the original Odd Couple, had formed a bond that mere clutter couldn't put asunder. Or so she hoped, as she filled up Kate's counters and tabletop with leftovers, frozen food, slightly wilted lettuce, just-right tomatoes, a nice hunk of imported Swiss cheese, a jar of olives, two cans of tuna fish, mixing bowls, frying pans, tinfoil, and knives.

Reaching for a box of rigatoni, she spotted Mary Frances and Billy standing in the dining area, staring at her, seemingly frozen, unable to cross the threshold.

"Come on in here. I have your assignments ready, but first, pour yourself a glass of wine, Mary Frances. I saw a nice Chablis in the fridge." She handed Billy his Shirley Temple, then pulled out a chair. "Sit right down at the table." Trying to sound maternal, she added, "Cheers, kid. Drink up. You're going to handle the hors d'oeuvres."

Billy ate the first of his cherries, appraised Marlene in silence, then sipped his drink, and nodded in approval.

"And what am I doing?" Mary Frances rummaged through the kitchen cabinets, reached for one of Kate's Waterford wine glasses, and poured the Chablis right up to its brim.

"Fill that big pot with water, add a teaspoon of salt, bring it to a boil, then add the rigatoni. While the water's boiling, open those two jars of spaghetti sauce, dump them into the other big pot, and I'll doctor it up. Since you're there at the stove, set the oven to three hundred and fifty degrees. We're having baked ziti, only with rigatoni as an understudy for ziti. And Swiss as a substitute for mozzarella." Marlene laughed. "Sort of like Annie Hall cooking Southern

Italian. But you work with what you've got."

"More, please." Billy pushed his empty glass toward Marlene.

"A little later. We need you sober, Billy, you have work to do." Marlene drained a jar of olives into a small bowl and lined up nine Ritz crackers on a plate. "Now watch, I'm cutting up these pieces of cheese. You'll put a piece of cheese on each cracker, then shove an olive onto one of these big toothpicks, and stick it through the cheese. Can you handle that, Billy?"

"Yes." He sounded almost happy.

Marlene checked out the spice rack—the same one Kate and Charlie had for decades in Rockville Centre—wondering how old the oregano was. In her own kitchen, she'd be able to judge shelf-age by the dust on the jar. No chance of that in Kate's overly clean kitchen.

With dinner perking along, and the smell of the canned sauce, jazzed up with basil and oregano and bits of deli ham, whetting her appetite, Marlene fixed Billy another Shirley Temple and poured herself another martini. Mary Frances, who hardly ever drank, was already on her second glass of wine.

"That's very artistic, Billy," Marlene said, meaning it. The plate of cheese and crackers was very tempting—though, of course, Marlene acknowledged she was easily tempted. "They look almost too good to eat."

"Sometimes I help my mommy."

Kate would have known how to parlay Billy's casual

comment into a Q-and-A session, but Marlene didn't have a clue.

"Do you and your mom eat dinner at home together every night?" Mary Frances asked.

He shrugged. "Sometimes. Sometimes we go to Denny's." His eyes filled with tears. "I want my mommy."

"Tell me about Denny's." Mary Frances sat down next to the boy and picked up a cracker. "What do you like to eat there?"

"Pancakes." Billy smiled. "I like them with syrup." Marlene remembered the doll lady saying the same thing earlier today about the House of Pancakes.

"For dinner?" Mary Frances asked.

"No, silly, for breakfast."

Mary Frances slipped the olive off the toothpick, plopped it on top of the cheese, and devoured the cracker in three tidy bites. "It's delicious, Billy. Do you want to try one?"

"I don't want that ugly green button."

Mary Frances removed the offending olive and gave Billy a topless cheese-and-cracker. He beat her record by a bite. She handed him another, then asked, "Does anyone ever go to Denny's with you and your mommy?"

"We go for breakfast with Uncle Carl when he stays overnight."

Nineteen

What in the world had gotten into Marlene and Mary Frances besides too many pre-dinner drinks? Not so unusual for Marlene, but Kate had never seen Mary Frances over-imbibe. You'd think with a child to mind, they might have been on better behavior.

Still . . . Kate felt touched by all the trouble the girls had gone to, creating a great meal out of nothing. She'd planned to treat everyone to dinner at the Neptune Inn, but this was much better. Billy, exhausted, would have never made it through the first course.

Obviously pleased to see Kate, the boy now clung to her side like an appendage, while petting Ballou who, in turn, tried to lick Billy's face.

While Marlene and Mary Frances were, indeed, acting very peculiarly, Kate realized they weren't tipsy, just on edge and cryptic. They kept giving her arch looks, as if expecting her to interpret their body language.

What the devil was going on?

Over coffee, Billy's head drooped, and Marlene whispered, "I'll fill you in after he's asleep." She stood and started to clear the table. "Go get him ready for bed. Mary Frances and I will clean up. Then we need to talk."

Both Marlene and Mary Frances kissed Billy goodnight. Kate watched him hug them back, taking great pleasure in the unlikely trio's interaction.

As Kate led Billy down the hall to the guest bathroom, she heard Mary Frances ask Marlene, "Did you tell her?"

Kate had her own news to share, but since hers painted Donna in such a bad light, she found herself far more intrigued by what Marlene and Mary Frances would have to report.

The ritual of bathing a child, helping him into his pajamas, and tucking him into bed stirred up old memories and current fears. To Kate's surprise, Billy, smelling like lavender soap and mint toothpaste, already knew "Now I Lay Me Down to Sleep." She kissed him good night, trying to keep a check on her maternal instincts. This boy belonged to another woman. A woman who could have killed his father.

She returned to the bathroom and splashed cold water on her eyes before heading back to the dining room.

"Where's Ballou?" Marlene sat at the cleared table, a yellow pad and pen in front of her, ready for business.

"Sleeping with Billy."

Marlene raised her eyebrows. "Is that recommended by Dr. Spock?"

"No," Kate snapped. "By me."

From the kitchen she could hear the dishwasher start, then Mary Frances calling out over its rumble, "I'll be right there."

"Don't you act snotty with me, Kate Kennedy." Marlene jabbed the pen in her direction. "While you've been out playing detective, I've been playing nanny, and doing a damn fine job of it."

"I'm sorry," Kate said, feeling her face flush and hot tears ready to roll again. "Really. And I appreciate everything you and Mary Frances have done." She swallowed hard, trying not to cry. "It's just that I'm frightened for Billy. I think his mother . . ."

"Might be a double murderer." Mary Frances finished Kate's sentence, then took a seat at the table.

Marlene glared at Mary Frances before turning to Kate. "Okay, apology accepted. Hey, I'm sorry, too. Let's get to work, before the flea market murders drive us all crazy."

"MonaLisa Buccino thinks Donna electrocuted Whitey Ford and then shot Carl Krieg because he could place her at Whitey's on Sunday night." Kate blurted the news out, twisting several strands of her short silver hair—a nervous habit she'd picked up decades ago when her hair had been long and the color of chestnuts.

"So do I." Mary Frances slapped the table. "And Donna may have had another reason to get rid of Carl."

"Billy told us," Marlene jumped in, stopping Mary Frances cold, "that *Uncle* Carl sometimes sleeps over, then takes mother and son out for breakfast. Now, isn't that cozy? You saw the size of her apartment."

Kate shook her head, thinking of Donna's close, if contentious relationship, with Sean Cunningham. Could she have been involved with three men?

"Who knows what multiple motives Donna had for shooting Carl? Sex adds a whole new dimension."

Mary Frances, the self-proclaimed virgin, spoke with great authority.

From any angle, an ugly mess. "If—and it's a big if—Donna did kill both men, we need to know why. Revenge? To collect on Whitey's insurance? He hadn't been paying child support? To cover up her animal abuse? To prevent Whitey from forwarding those photographs to the Humane Society? And what about that cut-up negative in her wastebasket?" Kate sighed, then rattled on. "Did she kill Carl because he knew she'd visited Whitey on Sunday night? Or were Whitey and Carl murdered—as Mary Frances suggests—because of Donna's very complicated romantic entanglements, which may include Sean? This morning in the bakery tent, I heard Sean warn Donna to keep her mouth shut about the abuse."

"Remember, Dolly told us Freddie's the photographer, not Whitey." Marlene stopped writing and frowned. "Maybe Whitey didn't take those pictures. But then why would he have made that phone call?"

"Right." Kate shook her head. "MonaLisa is convinced Freddie took the photographs and Whitey outright lied, wanting glory or to impress her. I'd vote for the latter. Whitey was a ladies' man, and MonaLisa's a beauty. I'm sure many men have tried to impress her. She believes that Whitey's lie led to his death and she feels guilty."

"Why should she feel guilty?" Mary Frances asked with great indignation. "Seems to me that Whitey Ford was a snake who got what he deserved."

Hang-'em-high Mary Frances. Yet another side of the dancing ex-nun.

"Well, Ford was no saint, that's for sure, but murder is never a form of justice." Kate sounded preachy. She really had to monitor these morality moments, but Mary Frances had pushed her FAIR PLAY button.

Marlene looked up from the yellow pad. "And we haven't even explored the other suspects. Remember how Sean attributed motives for Whitey's death to everyone in the corridor."

"Excluding himself and his brother Jocko." Kate laughed. It sounded small and tinny. "And today I overheard Freddie Ducksworth threaten Suzanna Jordan. Said he could provide eyewitness evidence that her daughter Olivia visited Whitey's apartment on the night he died. Apparently, Freddie was watching her from Carl Krieg's window. He claimed to not only be an eyewitness, but said he had photographs proving Olivia and Whitey were having an affair. Suzanna screamed, accusing Freddie of being a degenerate and a lying vulture."

"Incestuous little bunch of busy vendors, aren't they?" Marlene's raucous laughter filled the room. "Well, that might help explain Olivia's bizarre behavior in the corridor right before the fire—or what we all thought was a fire."

"What happened?" Mary Frances asked.

"Olivia kept rattling on about needing to find her mother, seemed nervous as hell. Said she'd received a note from Freddie, and she thought he was blackmailing her. Suzanna waltzed in and yelled 'Shut up, Olivia,' just as Ballou started barking, and Linda screamed, 'Fire!' "

For a moment, no one spoke.

Then Kate said, "And, as far as we know, Freddie Ducksworth's still among the missing."

"Jocko, too," Marlene said.

Mary Frances stood. "I'm going home, but there's one more thing we haven't addressed."

Probably a half-dozen things, Kate thought, feeling weary, wanting to sleep and think about all this tomorrow.

"Remember how Linda told us about Suzanna's car crash, and how it appeared to have been premeditated?" Mary Frances had Kate's full attention. "What if our theories and our motives are all wet? What if someone is plotting to murder all the corridor vendors? What if there's a serial killer in the flea market?"

Twenty

They'd decided to divide and conquer—Marlene off to Whitey Ford's memorial service, Kate to Broward General Hospital to visit Donna. That left Mary Frances to baby-sit Billy, neither adult nor child all that happy about spending the morning together.

The sun streamed through the double glass doors of Ocean Vista's lobby, its beams bouncing off the water in Aphrodite's fountain, the frolicking cupids bathed in its light.

Kate's mood was dark. Marlene hadn't arrived yet. And Mary Frances was pouting while Billy argued his case.

"I want to see my mommy. I am a big boy. The doctor will let me in. Please, please, Mrs. K." Billy spoke through tears, pointing at Mary Frances. "I don't want her to baby-sit me. I'm not a baby. I'm five."

"Well, there you go, Kate, I told you this wouldn't work." Mary Frances sounded pleased. *Humph.* If Mary Frances thought she'd just been relieved of duty, she had another think coming.

Kate knelt, her right knee cracking, her eyes level with Billy's. "I know, darling, you miss your mother." God, how she knew. The boy had wept his way through most of the night, finally falling asleep between Ballou and Kate, violating her own strict, no-Ballou-in bed rule. "I'll ask the doctor if you can visit your mother this afternoon. I promise, if he says yes, I'll bring you to see her."

"You promise?"

She nodded, ruffling his hair. "And I never break a promise."

His big blue eyes blinked, then Billy leaned in and whispered in Kate's ear, "But what will I do with her all day?"

A question Kate, on several occasions, had asked herself about Mary Frances. She giggled—it felt great—then whispered back, "Don't worry, Billy, I have a game plan for your play date with Miss Costello." Then she stood, almost losing her balance. Damn, getting up from a kneeling position got harder and harder.

"I heard that, Kate Kennedy. A play date? A game plan?" Mary Frances placed fisted hands on narrow hips, clad in the best-cut designer sweatpants Kate had ever seen. Navy blue French terry, piped in white, and topped with a matching jacket, its collar and zipper also trimmed in white. Covering up a bathing suit, Kate hoped.

"Aren't you too young to be getting so forgetful? We decided last night that you'd take Billy to Dinah's for pancakes." Kate spoke through clenched teeth. "That's his favorite breakfast. And the waitresses will just love him. Then you're going to the beach, right? And build a sand castle. If I'm not back by eleven, you're to take him to the pier and rent a fishing pole. Why are you acting as if all this is news to you?"

"Okay. Okay." Mary Frances pushed a stray red curl off her face, put on her sunglasses, and reached for the boy's hand. "Let's go."

Kate held her breath.

Billy smiled. "Pancakes." He grabbed Mary Frances's hand and waved at Kate. "Tell my mommy, 'see you later, alligator.'"

"Just remember I have a tango lesson at noon. So either you or Marlene had better be back here by eleven-thirty."

Kate exhaled as she watched them go out the front door. Dinah's, a Palmetto Beach landmark, was a short walk. A block north to Neptune Boulevard, then left toward the Intercoastal. The traffic lining up for the bridge to the mainland would be thick at this hour, but Kate knew Mary Frances would hold Billy's hand as they crossed the boulevard.

"Yo, Kate!" She turned and saw Marlene exiting the elevator and heading right toward the back door. "Do you want me to drop you at the hospital? It's on the way to the memorial."

"Please do not shout in the lobby," Miss Mitford scolded Marlene.

The condo president stuck out her tongue. Fortunately, the desk clerk had turned her attention to the pigeonholes behind her.

Kate craved solitude. She hurried to catch up with Marlene, who was holding the door to the parking lot open. "No, thanks. Mary Frances has issued an ultimatum. Kind of like *High Noon.* If I'm not back in time for her lesson, the tango champion will kill me."

Kate opened all four windows and drove down to Fort Lauderdale on A1A rather than I-95, counting on the ocean view to soothe her jangled nerves and hoping the salt air might clear her jumbled mind. If her hair frizzed, so be it. Kate *almost* believed one of the few pluses about the aging process was that most people seldom seemed to notice older women, so her hair, frizzed or smooth, was *almost* a non-issue.

Though the two-lane road made the trip longer, the highway wasn't an option. Not today. Lately, hardly ever, and Kate really didn't like to drive. She'd come of age in an era when many New York City women never learned to drive. If she and Charlie hadn't moved to the suburbs, she'd still be a nondriver. Her sons—and Charlie—had been telling her for years that she made a far better passenger than driver. She tended to agree with them; however, she had to get around, and South Florida had no subway system.

Besides, traveling at this slower pace, Kate could think.

Could Donna be as bad as the evidence indicated? A woman who abused animals? A woman who allowed Carl Krieg to stay overnight in that small apartment, while her son slept in the next room? A woman who seemed to want her ex-husband dead in order to collect his insurance money? A woman who shared dirty secrets with the sleazy Sean Cunningham? A woman who appeared to have embraced an immoral lifestyle and then flaunted it?

She'd better watch out: It was a short leap from a saintlike judgment call to a Salem-like witch burning.

Donna had raised Billy. Kate liked to think her two sons, good and decent men, reflected their mother's influence. Would Billy be such a good kid and loving son if Donna was such an evil woman? Would the child so desperately want to see his mother if she'd been abusive? Maybe. Some television self-help gurus thought so.

She'd visit Donna, form her up-close-and-personal opinion, then call Edmund. She admired Peter's partner, a well-respected, down-to-earth psychiatrist.

What is family for? Edmund wouldn't mind

answering a few questions about good and evil. And mother/son relationships.

Passing all the new, ornate, very expensive high-rise condos dotting the east side of A1A from Oakland Park to Fort Lauderdale, Kate wondered how anyone could afford them. It amazed and rather troubled her that so many people had so much money. Palmetto Beach, doggedly middle-class, now abutted some of the most expensive real estate in South Florida. If she and Ballou walked south, they'd be sharing the same sand, the same sea, and the same sunset with mega-millionaires.

She drove across the Sunrise Boulevard bridge, past the Galleria Mall, and the huge, well-stocked Borders where customers could dock their boats while they browsed through the book racks. Marlene and Kate often went to signings there or just hung out in the store's comfy chairs, reading, sipping café au lait, and watching the yachts anchor.

Turning south, she passed through Victoria Park, an area that looked more like New England than South Florida. With its cottages and Cape Cods, Wedgwood blue shutters, well-tended green lawns, and white picket fences, the neighborhood exuded charm and small-town appeal. Only the palm trees, rustling in the morning wind, reminded Kate that she was still in Fort Lauderdale.

The parking lot at Broward General Hospital appeared to be full, but in a far corner, at least the length of a city block away from the front entrance, she finally found a spot.

An elderly volunteer—elderly now defined as anyone ten years older than Kate—handed her a pass, saying, "Room 4122. Miss Viera already has a visitor, but since she's allowed two, you can go right on up, dear."

The lobby, somehow reminding Kate more of a hotel than a hospital, featured both a gift shop and a McDonald's. She bought a flowering plant in the former and two cups of hot tea—one for Donna, one for herself—in the latter.

Armed with her small gifts, she shared an elevator with a couple of nurses and two obviously very ill patients in wheelchairs, one a woman about Kate's age, one a boy about Billy's. The boy's bald head indicated he was receiving chemotherapy. She said a quick prayer. For the patients? Or because Billy and she weren't the patients. With the mental equivalent of a shrug, she decided to let God figure it out.

Outside Donna's room, she heard a man's voice and eavesdropped shamelessly. "If you talk, you're even crazier than I thought you were." Sean Cunningham sounded both threatening and a bit . . . what? . . . Frightened? "Don't say I didn't warn you, Donna."

"Get out of here, Sean, you're running late." Donna's voice was weak but icy. Kate strained to hear her. "And timing is everything for us circus performers, right? Like when the smoke bombs went off." Donna coughed, a raspy, scary sound. "Go to Whitey's memorial service, you old hypocrite. Light a candle for me."

Twenty-One

Why hadn't Kate wanted to ride with her? The memorial was at St. Anthony's, a couple of blocks from the hospital. Marlene wondered who'd picked the Fort Lauderdale church for the service. Whitey's parish, if he'd been a church-goer, would be in Palmetto Beach.

Had Sean Cunningham or one of Ford's corridor colleagues planned a reception after the service? She'd only had a quick cup of coffee and a stale, half-toasted bagel at dawn—well, seven-thirty, but way too early for Marlene, who like Count Dracula and the Phantom of the Opera preferred the music of the night. A spread— maybe lox and cream cheese and fresh bagels in the church hall—would be most welcome. More important, by mixing with the mourners, she could field questions without appearing too pushy.

If not, she'd just have to grab people in the vestibule and fire away.

Over the years, Marlene had made the arrangements for far too many funerals, the price paid for outliving so many loved ones. She'd never planned a memorial service without a food-filled reception following. Would the circus crowd be as hospitable?

Kate once had told Marlene that St. Anthony's reminded her of a traditional Northern church. So many South Florida churches were modern, their architectural design as airy and light as a beach resort, their stained glass windows done in pastels. Whenever Kate, who put great faith in St. Anthony—revered for finding lost objects—needed to do some serious praying, she often bypassed her parish church, St. Elizabeth's, and drove down to St. Anthony's.

"Blimey, Marlene, don't you look like mourner-in-chief?" Linda Rutledge called out as Marlene entered the last pew. "Come on, let's go sit down front where we can see all the action."

Marlene, who'd gone to great trouble to dress appropriately for Whitey Ford's memorial, took umbrage at Linda's remark. Yes, she was wearing a tailored, black, lightweight wool pants suit and, for her, sensible shoes—sling-backs, closed toes—but she hardly looked like a grieving widow.

Nevertheless, she nodded and followed the doll lady, dressed in aqua satin and a matching cartwheel straw hat the size of a bicycle tire, down the aisle.

The front pews were packed. The circus performers and crew had come out in force. The colorfully clad entertainers and the tattooed, tough-talking roustabouts had turned into an eclectic congregation.

"I always sit on the bride's side." Linda gestured left, and they slid into seats about ten rows back from the altar.

Directly in front of them sat Jocko Cunningham, no longer among the missing. Indeed, this morning the clown was scrubbed up, smelling of cologne, and dressed in a dark suit and tie. He knelt, head bowed, apparently deep in prayer.

Marlene tapped his shoulder. Jocko jumped, then

jerked his head around. "Oh, it's you, Ms. Friedman, you startled me."

More like she'd terrified him. Feeling that she had the advantage, she plunged. "We thought you were dead, Jocko. From the smoke. Or maybe murdered like Carl. Where were you? When I left the corridor yesterday, the firefighters were still searching for you and Freddie Ducksworth."

His pale face flushed. Beads of sweat broke out across his forehead. "Haven't I just been thanking God for sparing me?" Jocko yanked a handkerchief out of his breast pocket—to Marlene's surprise, it was both clean and ironed—and wiped his brow. "I helped get the elephants out, but I knew I couldn't handle the tigers and went searching all over for their trainer. I finally located Jim, and together we got the tigers into their portable cages. The smoke was fierce. I remember wondering why there weren't any flames. I could hardly breathe, so a sweeper and Jim wheeled the tigers over to the animal exit. I ran back into the elephants' pen looking for a cloth to cover my mouth and nose. Some bastard—oh—forgive my cursing in church— locked me in. A firefighter found me facedown in the straw and rescued me."

"You were okay?" Marlene heard the doubt in her voice.

"Well, of course, he was," Linda snapped. "He's here, isn't he?"

Jocko met Marlene's gaze. "They wanted to take me to Broward County's emergency room, Ms. Friedman,

to be treated for smoke inhalation, but I refused to go."
Cold. Marlene had made an enemy.

Organ music filled the church and a deep baritone
voice sang, "Ave Maria."

Enemy or not, Marlene boldly spoke over the hymn's
words and music. "Did you see the man's face? The one
who locked you in the cage?"

"No, Ms. Friedman, I didn't." Jocko shook his head,
his jowls, an unfortunate Cunningham family trait,
shaking. "At the time, I was busy vomiting into a rag."
He turned his back and returned to the knee rail.

Marlene didn't believe the clown's story. But even
if he'd lied about his heroics, someone had apparently locked him in the elephants' cage. Who? And
why?

Across the aisle—on the groom's side—a sobbing
Olivia sat slumped against her mother, the latter rigid
and aloof. Suzanna Jordan made Snow White's wicked
stepmother seem warm and fuzzy. The daughter struck
Marlene as overly needy and probably clinically
depressed, but the mother's lack of response bordered
on contempt.

Had Freddie Ducksworth really been blackmailing
Olivia? Had sad-sack Olivia killed Whitey? If she'd
been in love—or even believed herself to be in love
with the older man and Whitey had rejected her, could
such a timid soul have committed murder? Maybe. A
crime of passion was one thing, but Carl Krieg's death
had been premeditated murder. It would have taken a
cold-blooded killer to pull that off. A personality more

like Suzanna's than Olivia's. Or a personality like Donna Viera's. Or Sean Cunningham's. Or Freddie Ducksworth's. Or Linda Rutledge's. Lots of overbearing people had worked the corridor, including the two dead men.

The doll lady sighed as the priest sprinkled holy water while circling Whitey Ford's picture, which stood on a small table, along with a tall vase of white roses, in front of the communion rail.

No casket. No urn. No remains to be sprinkled. Ford's body, now tagged evidence, was in the morgue, scheduled for an autopsy.

Marlene put on her distance glasses and focused on Whitey's photograph. Handsome man, with smiling, sexy eyes. According to this morning's *Sun-Sentinel*, Whitey had donated his body to science, so there'd be no burial either.

Sean Cunningham strode down the aisle and up to the pulpit to deliver the eulogy. When had he arrived?

"Heaven has a new resident," Sean began, in a sad, but stage-trained boom.

"And hell awaits you!" Olivia screamed from her pew.

Twenty-two

Kate crossed the threshold and a plastic pitcher filled with water came flying her way. She ducked. Donna had a powerful arm; the pitcher sailed over Kate's head and landed in the hallway.

"Damn. I thought you were that snake, Sean, slithering back in."

Kate picked up the pitcher, stepped into the tiny bathroom to grab a towel, then silently mopped up the water. An unsuspecting nurse could slip, fall, and land in the empty bed next to Donna.

"So, okay, I'm sorry." Kate would bet that the only thing Donna felt sorry about was having missed Sean's skull.

The broken leg—in a cast up to Donna's hip and suspended from a sci-fi contraption—had to hurt like hell. Still, the pain etched on her face seemed to emanate from older, deeper wounds, and not the kind caused by physical injury.

"How's Billy?" The anger dissipated, if only for a moment. "Why didn't you bring him?" Not even a thank-you for taking care of her little boy. How had this asocial creature taught her son such good manners? And to say his evening prayers?

"He's fine, Donna. He misses you." Kate said. "I just wanted to be sure the hospital would allow a five-year-old to visit. If we get permission, I'll bring him this afternoon."

"I might be under arrest by then."

"What?" Kate sank into a chair next to the bed, the smell of disinfectant stronger now, almost overwhelming. "Why?" Her heart couldn't race any faster if one of her granddaughters was about to go to jail.

"For the murder of Carl Krieg." Donna's irises looked as black as her pupils. With puffy lids and dark circles, she seemed to have aged ten years overnight. Her fingers fluttered across the frayed cotton binding on a white blanket, covering her good leg and upper body. "That Detective Carbone either found some—er—evidence or he listened to a bunch of dirty lies." Fear filled her swollen eyes. "How could he believe such garbage?"

Did you do it, Donna? Kate felt bold enough and curious enough to ask the question but couldn't get the words out. Maybe she wasn't prepared to hear the answer.

"I didn't, you know." Eerie. Had Kate been that transparent? "Why would I kill my uncle? This is South Florida, for God's sake, not some drafty castle in Denmark."

The *Hamlet* allusion surprised Kate, but it shouldn't have. The enigmatic Donna had proved to be a study in contrasts from the moment they'd met.

"So Carl Krieg was your uncle?" Kate hoped her neutral tone masked her skepticism.

"Yes, a great-uncle on my mother's side. Carl was my grandmother's brother."

Kate nodded, waiting. She sat very still, not wanting to distract Donna.

"My grandmother, Greta, and her brother, Carl, grew up in Brazil. They'd moved there from Germany as children right after World War Two."

So Kate's Hitler's Youth guess had been on target.

"Lots of Germans settled in Rio in the late forties. My great-grandfather had been an SS officer, but Uncle

Carl was okay. More than okay. He helped me out financially when I moved down here from New Bedford, and he really loved Billy."

Took his great-great-nephew out for pancakes, Kate thought.

"Grandmother Greta married a Brazilian, and her only daughter married my father, Antonio Viera. A handsome devil. They migrated to the U.S. and settled in New Bedford. Mom died of breast cancer when I was twelve, and my father, a fisherman, died in a shipwreck a few weeks before my eighteenth birthday. I was bored, lonely, and tired of the cold weather, so I moved down here." Donna stopped abruptly as if worn out.

"Don't talk," Kate said, hoping Donna would continue.

"No. Someone murdered my Uncle Carl. I want to tell you about him. About me. When I arrived in Florida, I lived with him for awhile. That's how I met Whitey. And Whitey and Carl introduced me to Sean. And the next thing I knew, some old animal trainer—about to be put out to pasture by the Cunninghams—taught me the ropes, and before I turned twenty, I had an elephant act."

"Would you like a glass of water?" Kate asked.

Donna ignored Kate's offer, and continued. "Until yesterday, except for my son, Carl Krieg was my only living relative in the entire United States. Now all I have is Billy."

Yesterday, she'd said something very similar—"there's no one left"—as she begged Kate to care for

Billy. Had that been a reference to Uncle Carl's recent murder? Probably.

Donna shifted her position, then grimaced. "Damn. I can't even move an inch without my leg hurting like hell." Tears glistened, hovered on her lashes, and fell in a steady stream down her cheeks.

Kate handed her a box of tissues and, though tempted to reach out and touch Donna's slim shoulder, remained in her chair, silently paraphrasing Milton: We also serve who only *sit* and wait.

She didn't have to wait long.

"My uncle used to sit like a sentinel, drinking scotch and watching the passing parade of tenants and their guests going in and out of the building." The young woman sighed. Resigned? Forlorn? "Carl was at his post Sunday evening. That skunk, Whitey, had a record number of visitors on the night he drew his fatal bath."

"Could Carl have told one of those visitors?" In her excitement, Kate's question just popped out. She hadn't even realized she'd spoken aloud until Donna laughed.

"One of them? Uncle Carl was a card-carrying drunk, Mrs. Kennedy. A drunk who'd show up at my house on a Friday night, drink like a demon, then pass out on my couch. And I'd have to sleep on a futon. He'd be all apologies the next morning and insist on treating Billy and me to a big breakfast."

Hell's bells! Maybe Carl had cut up that negative and dropped the pieces in Donna's wastebasket.

"When he drank, he talked. Uncle Carl blabbed to

every single one of them—all suspects—almost like he had a death wish."

"Who were they?"

Donna tried to adjust her blanket. "God almighty, I can't stand the pain. Ring for the nurse, Mrs. Kennedy."

"Can you give me the names?" Feeling guilty for pressuring the patient, Kate pressed the CALL button.

"I gave their names to Detective Carbone. And I'm still his odds-on favorite." Donna shook her head. "Look, the time line's hazy. Carl kept changing the order of arrivals and departures. I think one or two might have overlapped, but Whitey's visitors were Sean, Linda, Olivia, and Suzanna."

Based on his threat to Suzanna, the now-missing Freddie Ducksworth had been at Carl's apartment that night, snapping pictures through the front window. Had Freddie dropped by Whitey's, too?

"And what about you, Donna, where were you on Sunday night?"

The patient groaned. "Mrs. Kennedy, I don't give a flying fig what you think about me. But even if you believe I'm a cold-blooded killer, you have to promise me you'll take care of Billy."

For today? For a week? Forever? Kate stared at Billy's mother.

"Promise me!"

"I promise," Kate said, as Nick Carbone skidded though a small puddle she must have missed and landed on his knees at her feet.

Twenty-three

Kate felt deliciously wicked. She'd left Nick Carbone in the emergency room at Broward General waiting to have his old "trick" knee X-rayed. With six far more seriously injured patients ahead of him, Carbone wouldn't be arresting anyone for a while. Though to be fair, between yelps of pain—men can be such big babies—he explained that he'd only dropped by the hospital to ask Donna a few more questions. Well, those questions would just have to wait, wouldn't they?

The detective's tumble had given Kate a head start. She had places to go and people to see if she wanted to prove Billy's mother wasn't a double murderer.

She'd left Nick in midsentence, sputtering, "I'm warning you, Kate, don't get . . ."

Waving good-bye, she'd dashed out of the emergency room, not feeling the least bit sorry that Detective Carbone would be out of action, at least for a couple of hours. As soon as she hit the lobby, she called Jeff Stein at the *Palmetto Beach Gazette* and made a date with him for lunch at one o'clock.

Maybe she'd accept Jeff's freelance job offer and try her hand at a feature article. Certainly, they could discuss that. But her real mission was to see if Donna had ever called him about his animal-abuse article and to find out what Jeff knew about Sean Cunningham's and Whitey Ford's past lives. Kate had a hunch they'd been intertwined.

As she pulled into Ocean Vista's parking lot, her gloating over Carbone and her suspicions about Cunningham came to an abrupt halt, replaced by a paradox: Donna's overzealous prodding of an elephant, and Billy, so proud of his mother, gleefully recounting riding on one.

Act as if, Kate. Prove Donna's innocence for Billy's sake. Now that challenge could be a real paradox. She stepped out of the car, and into a warm breeze, laughing at herself.

"Miss Costello and that child," Miss Mitford managed to turn *child* into an obscenity, "have gone up to her apartment. She'd like you to join them there."

"Thanks."

Kate crossed the lobby and rang for the south elevator, wondering if she could take the *child* and Ballou on her appointed rounds and, if not, would Marlene be back in time to mind Billy and walk the Westie.

Mary Frances lived in 730, a one-bedroom apartment with a southern exposure and a nice view of the ocean.

The former nun had transformed her only bedroom into a dance studio, complete with a raised parquet floor, ballet barre, and sound system. Three of the walls were mirrored. The fourth was covered with clothes racks, filled with colorful costumes, baskets brimming with castanets, and open shoe boxes, lined up like soldiers, holding sexy high-heel pumps matching both the costumes and the castanets. Even more amazing, somehow Mary Frances had charmed the previous condo board into approving the changes.

Kate rapped sharply. No answer. She tried the door, and it opened. A Latin beat emanated from the former bedroom, literally filling the wall-to-wall-dolls living room. She crossed the room, went down a small hall, its bookcases housing Mary Frances's Henry the VIII and his wives collection, and peered into the dance studio.

Billy, standing tall and straight and grinning from ear to ear, had one arm thrust forward, leading Mary Frances in what appeared to be a smooth, well-rehearsed tango.

Feeling a bit jealous, Kate applauded their performance.

"Hi, Mrs. K." Billy danced over to her. "Can I go with Mary Frances to her tango lesson? Please! She wants to take me." His blue eyes sparkled. A sparkle missing since his mother had been injured. A sparkle that the dancing ex-nun rather amazingly had restored.

Well, Mary Frances's tango lesson might solve Kate's baby-sitting problem. Marlene could be stuck at Whitey's memorial or, putting a more positive spin on her absence, be busy gathering information from the mourners after the service.

Kate hugged Billy, then locked eyes with Mary Frances. "Are you sure?"

"Sure?" Mary Frances removed the rose from her teeth. "You bet I'm sure. I've had more fun today teaching Billy to tango than I ever had during my thirty-year career as a nun."

With some unexpected time on her hands, but not wanting to get sand in her shoes, Kate took Ballou for a quick walk on A1A. The Westie turned north toward Neptune Boulevard, and she followed his lead.

As he strutted ahead, Kate's cell phone rang. Her granddaughter and namesake, Katharine. Drat. Not that she wasn't thrilled to hear from her favorite person in the entire world—now that Charlie had moved on—but she disliked chatting on the phone in public. She'd overheard far too many private, intimate, or even angry conversations between taxi drivers and their significant others, while a virtual prisoner in a cab's backseat. Trapped, seat belt buckled, waiting for the plane to take off, she'd been forced to listen as total strangers across the aisle spilled out their guts or their sex lives. And, on the beach, teenagers shouted vulgar words and crude jokes into their cell phones, seemingly unaware that they were loud enough to be heard in Fort Lauderdale.

"Hi, Katharine." She spoke into the transmitter.

"How you doing, Nana?"

"Fine, I guess. Keeping busy."

With her red hair and freckles, and short, solid body, her younger granddaughter reminded Kate so much of Charlie. She had her grandfather's spark, too. Lauren, the Harvard pre-med student, was more like her mother's family, the Lowell's. Tall, rangy, blonde and, for Kate's taste, a bit bland.

Charlie had nicknamed his son's in-laws the Boston Bores.

"Well, get the guest room ready, Nana, I'm flying down Saturday morning. Just for the weekend. I'll play hooky on Monday. All the discount airlines are having a price war. At forty-nine dollars each way, how could I resist?"

"Er."

"Nana?" Kate heard the hurt in Katharine's voice.

"That would be grand, darling. Come on down!"

She'd figure out the sleeping arrangements later. Maybe either Katharine or Billy could stay at Marlene's.

"Is your sister coming, too?"

"Hell, no, Nana. Lauren's in lust. Again. This time with a Nob Hill Brahmin. Daddy says he's a stuffed shirt. Lauren says Daddy has no appreciation for the finer things in life. Mom says Daddy does so, he married her, didn't he?"

Kate laughed. Score one for Jennifer. She and Kevin, despite their very different backgrounds and very different careers—he a firefighter, she a stockbroker—were still madly in love after twenty-three years of marriage.

"Okay, darling, I'll see you Saturday." She fleetingly thought of telling Katharine about Billy, but decided to wait. "E-mail your flight information, and Auntie Marlene and I will pick you up." Kate sighed. "Or it might just be me and a little surprise package, if the flea market corridor reopens before Saturday."

"I'm sure there's some sense in what you just said, Nana, but you can explain it to me when I get there.

Love you a bunch. Bye."

On Neptune Boulevard, Ballou veered west toward the bridge. He probably wanted to stop at Dinah's, the last coffee shop in South Florida that permitted small pets to accompany their mostly senior masters.

"Sorry, Ballou, this is a business trip." She waved the pooper-scooper and small Baggie under his nose. "So do yours, I have to get going."

"Kate, is that you?"

She spun around and saw MonaLisa and Tippi approaching them from the east. Tippi once again dropped to her stomach and eyed Ballou, who sniffed, straining to reach Tippi's nose and other body parts.

MonaLisa ran her hand through her hair. "Oh, God, Kate, have you heard the news?" She sounded harried and, in the bright midday light, looked drawn.

"What?" Kate reached out and touched the younger woman's arm. "What's wrong, MonaLisa?"

"The police found Freddie Ducksworth's body, apparently last night, but they just announced it now. I heard it on *News at Noon*."

Kate shivered in the sunshine. "Where?"

"At the circus. In the elephant area, stuffed into a crate where they keep the feed." MonaLisa gulped. "It looks like a big coffin."

"Shot." Not a question. Kate was certain.

"Through the head. Just like Carl."

Twenty-four

Sean Cunningham proved to be a cheapskate as well as a snake. No reception for poor Whitey. Not even an invitation to stop for a good-bye toast at one of the many bars or restaurants within walking distance on Las Olas.

"You'd think that tightwad would stand us to a round of drinks, but no such luck," Linda said, gesturing to a small yellow sports car. "Follow me home, Marlene. I live on Harborage Isle. We need to have a little chat, don't we? I'll have my houseboy scrape up some lunch, then you and I can have a couple of champagne cocktails out on the terrace overlooking the Intercoastal and give poor Whitey a proper sendoff."

Harborage Isle? Probably the priciest real estate in Fort Lauderdale. A houseboy serving lunch? Champagne cocktails on the terrace? Linda would have to sell a hell of a lot of Queen Annes to afford that lifestyle. The doll lady must have another source of really big bucks.

Marlene called Kate, leaving messages on both her home and cell phones, saying she wouldn't be home for lunch, but she hoped Kate would make Mary Frances's noon deadline.

She followed Linda's yellow convertible—Italian, she thought, maybe a Ferrari, but without her reading glasses, she couldn't be sure—east on Las Olas toward the ocean, then south on A1A.

The beach—so close to the road along the Fort Lauderdale strip, Marlene felt as if she could reach out the window and touch the ocean—was packed with college students, celebrating an annual rite of passage: spring break.

Beautiful bodies lay supine on colorful towels spread across the sand, soaking up the sun. Young women in bikinis and tankinis dipped painted toenails into the surf. Young men with pumped-up muscles played volleyball. The surfers, always ready, stood with their boards erect, keeping one eye on the waves and the other on the girls.

As she drove past the T-shirt shops, the old seedy bars, the new upscale boutiques, and the landmark Yankee Clipper Hotel, she decided that Fort Lauderdale was now, and always had been, more than just a tourist trap. The city, like the state, represented growth and change, sleaze and style and, even hidden under its glamour and grit, Southern charm.

"Where the Boys Are," Marlene sang aloud, remembering all the words to the theme song from the quintessential spring-break movie. What a mad crush she'd had on George Hamilton. One of many youthful crushes that now made her cringe and wonder, what was she thinking?

She laughed . . . as if lust had anything to do with logic.

It would have been easy to miss the turn off A1A leading to the bridges to Harborage Isle. The residents of that exclusive area didn't encourage either tourists or local gawkers. If Marlene hadn't been tailing Linda, she'd have sailed right by.

After crossing several bridges with isles off each, Linda drove through tall black gates, instructing the uniformed guard to allow Marlene to follow her into the enclave. *Awesome,* like *amazing,* had become an overused adjective, mostly uttered by dithering contestants on reality shows like *The Bachelor,* but with no exaggeration, the stunning homes on Harborage Isle truly awed and amazed Marlene.

Her hostess pulled into the circular Moroccan tile driveway of what Marlene decided might be best described as a mansion. Old money had built this baby. Not much property, but then its backyard abutted the Intercoastal. A good-sized, bright green front lawn, surrounded by a wall of hydrangea bushes and graced with two royal palm trees, led to a porch with white double doors. A mini-Tara.

An Arab butler, complete with turban, opened the front door before Linda had time to either fumble for a key or knock. The foyer with its twelve-foot ceiling housed bookcases filled with Linda's *Gone With the Wind* doll collection, including a lifelike Scarlett O'Hara in her mother's green velvet drapes. The Arab butler came as a surprise; Rhett Butler did not.

"Good morning, Omar. It is still morning, isn't it?"

"It is, indeed, madame." A slight accent and a deep sexy voice. He nodded at Marlene.

"Ms. Friedman will be joining us for lunch. On the terrace. Lemon sole, I think. And a goat cheese salad."

Us? Marlene pondered the meaning of "us."

"Very good, madame." The butler turned and smiled at Marlene, his teeth gleaming like a toothpaste ad. "Welcome to Xanadu, Ms. Friedman."

So the modest mansion had a name. How *tres* South of France for South Florida.

"And we'll start with champagne cocktails, just as quickly as you can pop the cork." Linda swept into the sunken living room, bathed in sunlight and furnished with Middle Eastern treasures.

By the second round, served in crystal flutes on a silver tray, Linda was Marlene's new best friend.

A motor yacht sailed by, the captain waving at them from the helm.

The multilevel terrace—with an Olympic-size pool on one level—sloped down to the Intercoastal. From their table, Marlene could almost reach out and shake the captain's hand.

Where had all this money come from? The lady of the house didn't strike Marlene as being to the manor born. Just how much could she get out of Linda? In South Florida, polite people didn't pry into acquaintances' previous lives. Former drug lords and white-collar criminals had too often morphed into knights in shining armor, endowing libraries and building opera houses. Should she start by confiding in Linda, establishing trust? Rapport? Hell, she didn't time for subtleties.

She chuckled, like she'd ever been subtle.

"Something strike your funny bone, Marlene?"

"Just reflecting on my checkered past." Not bad for openers.

Linda gazed at her, long and hard. Her hostess had changed into a gauzy white caftan, pulled her hair back in a ponytail and wiped off her makeup, saying she wanted to work on her tan. Even in the bright sunlight, the doll lady appeared years younger.

"You do remind me a bit of my old mum."

Not exactly what Marlene had expected—or wanted—to hear. Well, of course, Linda was young enough to be her daughter, but she had trouble picturing herself as anyone's "mum."

"Really?" Marlene tried to sound flattered.

"Drove me away from home, the old tart did."

"Oh . . ."

"Slept her way through Liverpool, didn't she?" Linda winked. "The twig doesn't fall far from the tree, does it?"

Again, aping her sister-in-law, Marlene merely nodded.

"I quit school at sixteen, ran away from that ugly counsel house, and married a strung-out rocker— thought he looked like the reincarnation of John Lennon. Came over here to the States with him. But he left me for the drummer, who, odd enough, looked uncannily like Ringo Starr."

Linda paused, then drained and refilled her flute. "Another?"

Knowing she had to drive home, Marlene said, "Yes, please." What the hell, she'd drink a lot of coffee.

"So there I was, stranded in Sarasota."

Marlene started, thinking of the midget. "I . . . er . . . once had a fling in Sarasota."

"Not much else to do there, is there?" Linda twirled the ends of her ponytail. "Lunch should be ready soon."

"What did you do after he left you?" To her surprise, Marlene was genuinely interested.

"Got a job in the circus, then bounced around Florida, and moved to Fort Lauderdale, about fifteen years ago. I got a job at the Silver Swizzle, became the club's hottest lap dancer." Linda shrugged. "Long story short—I landed in the lap of luxury. Married a Texas oilman. I adored George. We had a wonderful life, like the movie, only we were bloody rich, didn't need an angel. He bought this house for me. A Saudi prince had lived here. Try the bathroom off the living room. Mirrored walls. Mirrored floors. Mirrored ceiling. Absolutely decadent. You'll see parts of your body you never knew you had. Anyway, the butler was part of the deal. I didn't ask any questions. My dearest love died five years ago. Heart attack. I met Sean at Ireland's Inn shortly after George's death. I loved dolls, and I desperately needed something to do. The flea market and Precious saved my life."

"Where is Precious?"

"At Kitty Korner having her weekly shampoo and pedicure. Omar will bring her home later."

"I guess the flea market will never be the same." Marlene's venture wasn't the smoothest segue, but she felt

137

tipsy herself and hoped the champagne would keep Linda talking,

"Whitey Ford, charming toad that he was, set the flea market on its heels long before this mess."

According to Sean, Whitey had dumped Linda. Her judgment might be skewed.

Damn this tiptoeing around. Full speed ahead. "Do you think Whitey was murdered because he discovered that Suzanna's car crash hadn't been an accident?"

"That could one of several motives. Maybe a motive for Olivia. You know, given the right opportunity, I might have killed my mum."

Why had Linda singled out Olivia? And what other motives did the doll lady have in mind? "Strange how Olivia lashed out at Sean in church this morning. Yesterday, he told Kate and me the girl had a crush on Whitey."

"More than a crush. Ask Freddie, he has the photographs to prove it." Linda smirked. "But he has other incriminating pictures, as well, hasn't he?"

The butler, silent as a cat, appeared at Linda's side. "Madame, I just heard on the telly in the kitchen that Mr. Ducksworth is dead." He paused. "And I gather not from natural causes."

Good God! Suddenly, Mary Frances's earlier theory about all the vendors being targets no longer seemed so bizarre. Maybe there really was a serial killer in the flea market.

Twenty-five

Kate believed the best bagel in South Florida—or, at least, to a New York purist, the taste that came closest to the real thing—could be purchased at Einstein's Bagels located on Federal Highway near an Italian gourmet deli with great homemade ravioli. Two delicious reminders of home in one strip mall.

She and her fellow former New Yorker, Jeff Stein, the editor of the *Palmetto Beach Gazette*, met at Einstein's every Sunday morning. First by accident, then by design. She missed her sons. He missed his mother. So, on Sunday mornings, they met, they talked, they ate, almost like family.

Today was Thursday, but a bagel and a schmear still seemed to be in order. Einstein's weekday customers, mostly office workers on lunch break, ate much faster than the Sunday-morning regulars, who tended to chat with each other or read their newspapers. Right now, the bagel shop's turnaround time averaged about ten minutes, so Jeff and Kate found a tiny table for two in the back, hoping not to be disturbed.

"I wanted some history on Whitey Ford and Sean Cunningham and what Carl Krieg might have found out that got him murdered. But now that Freddie's dead, too, I don't know where to begin." Kate spoke as she spread strawberry cream cheese to the outer limits of her plain, but not toasted, bagel. Einstein's bagels were too fresh to toast.

"Let's start with the latest victim and work our way back." Jeff, in khakis, pale blue shirt, and a neatly knotted tie—the latter unusual for anyone other than bankers, financial planners, or con men in South Florida—smiled. He had an easy charm, a quick, fertile mind, and tweedy good looks, like a youngish professor who'd removed his jacket. "Want to try some of my cream cheese with chives?"

"No way," Kate laughed. "Strawberry is as far as I deviate from tradition."

"I knew Ducksworth." Jeff said around a bite of bagel. "Great collection of comic books."

"Are you a collector, Jeff?" Kate again thought of her sons and how they—though they'd swear to the contrary—had never completely forgiven her for throwing out their Marvel comics.

"Yeah, I am." He blushed. "Since I bought so many first editions from Freddie—he was great about special orders—I had a nodding acquaintance with all the vendors in the corridor."

"Good." Kate nodded. "Your impressions of that bunch can only help me fill in the blanks." She pressed a Twining English Breakfast tea bag against her spoon and squeezed it into her large mug, so the wet bag wouldn't drip. With no saucer, she laid the spoon on a paper napkin, watching Jeff grin at her fussiness.

"Are you going to write a story for me, or are you just playing detective, Kate?" She heard a slight edge of sarcasm in his voice.

"It's not that I don't want to write, I just don't know if I can."

"That obit you wrote was damn good. Try a feature article, Kate. If it's lousy, I'm not shy, I won't use it."

She lifted her head and met Jeff's eyes. "Okay, I'll write about the flea market murders. And I'll write about the animal abuse." The passion of her commitment surprised her; it felt right, like she really could be a newspaper reporter. Hell's bells, at least she could try.

"Freddie struck me as an opportunist." Jeff moved the conversation back on track. "And not above bending the law. When you told me he'd tried to blackmail the Jordan mother and daughter team, I can't say I was surprised. I've spent the last hour adding to what I already knew about all the vendors."

"And?" Kate felt a tingle. The same sort of tingle she'd gotten all those years ago while reading Agatha Christie and trying to guess the murderer before Miss Marple did.

"When Ducksworth was twenty-two, he spent a year in jail in Kansas, where he grew up. For a check scam involving old ladies. Though he hasn't been in trouble with the law since then, a recent customer has been making noise about suing Freddie over a phony first edition of *The Phantom*. Caused quite a stir in comic-book circles."

"You believe Freddie *deliberately* turned his photography hobby into a blackmailing scheme."

"Well, yes. Come on, Kate, when it quacks, walks,

and looks like a duck—pun intended—it's probably Ducksworth."

"Really bad pun." Kate laughed. "Okay. So Freddie was murdered because he'd taken those photographs of Whitey's final visitors' arrivals and departures." Kate's voice expressed her doubt.

Jeff shrugged. "Don't you think?"

"What about the animal abuse? Maybe the killer wanted to prevent proof of the mistreated elephants from arriving at the Humane Society."

"Kate, that motive for Freddie's death makes no sense. Whitey called, saying he'd send the photographs, not Freddie."

"MonaLisa Buccino, who investigated the abuse, never believed that Whitey shot those photos. Maybe the killer knew Freddie had taken them."

Jeff drained his coffee cup. "If the abuse photographs were the motive, why wouldn't Freddie have been the first victim, not the third?"

"Who killed Whitey and why?" Kate sighed. "Two people may have been murdered because they knew the answer to that question."

"Since we're working backward, let's look at victim number two, Carl Krieg." Jeff stood. "Let me get another cup of coffee."

"And tea for me, please." Kate glanced at her watch. Twelve forty-five. Good. She planned to fetch Billy at two and take him to see Donna. She had a message on her cell phone from Marlene—who must have called while she'd been talking to Katharine. Wondering how the memorial service had gone and what Marlene would learn from Linda, she finished the last of her bagel and started on her fruit cup.

Jeff placed a fresh mug of hot water and another tea bag in front of Kate. "Go ahead, do your neat thing."

"Then Carl died because Freddie shot those pictures from his front window. An eyewitness once removed." Kate finished her tea-bag brewing ritual. "That narrows our suspect list to four. According to Donna, Carl said Whitey's visitors were Sean, Linda, Olivia, and Suzanna. Unfortunately, Carl was a drunk and couldn't be sure of the time line."

"If we could find the photos, Kate, we'd have the time line." Jeff shook his head. "I'll bet the killer has them."

"What did you find out about Carl?"

"Well, as you know, he was Donna's uncle. And he and Jocko—real name Joseph—Cunningham have been active members, for years, in a local bund. In Davie."

"Bund? You mean like the groups that Nazi sympathizers joined just before America entered World War Two?" Kate felt repulsed.

Jeff nodded. "Exactly." He looked bleak. "I don't know how—or if—that tidbit ties into the murders, but those are the ugly facts, ma'am."

"What about the four visitors? We know Suzanna's motive—to protect her daughter. And Olivia's— unrequited love—or maybe a romantic fling, followed by rejection if Whitey rebuffed her advances.

But what about Linda and Sean?"

"Those two share a long and interesting history, Kate. Linda worked as a lap dancer in the Silver Swizzle, a men's-only club that Sean owned. The doll lady met her husband there. But before the oil baron, she'd danced in Whitey's lap. That's how their love affair began."

Twenty-six

"Son of a b—"

"Marlene, lower your voice, Billy will hear you."

Catching their breath and a few rays of the early afternoon sun on Kate's balcony before leaving for the hospital, they'd traded tales of their respective investigations. Revelations of Linda's duplicity had driven Marlene to foul language.

"That lying witch," Marlene sputtered, "she played me like putty."

"What intrigues me is why Linda lied. Why should it matter how many years ago she met Sean and Whitey? Or where? Why would meeting Sean at Ireland's Inn after her husband's death be okay, but not at the Silver Swizzle, which Sean owned. She'd admitted to dancing there. And to an affair with Whitey." Kate brushed a stray silver hair out of her eye. "I wonder if Linda knows that Sean already told us about her and Whitey. Of course, he implied their romance had been more recent."

"Maybe," Marlene almost shouted, "the affair *was* recent. Maybe it never ended. Maybe Linda and Whitey were sleeping together all through her deliriously happy marriage to George."

"Is it time to go see my mommy?" Billy stood in the open door leading to Kate's balcony, Ballou at his side. The dog ran over for a quick pat from both Kate and Marlene.

"Yes, darling, it's time." Kate stood. "And if Auntie Marlene promises to behave, she can come with us."

They drove down A1A in Marlene's 1957 white Chevy convertible with the top down. Billy, all smiles, dubbed the car "neat." Donna must say "neat," meaning so much more than nice. Or could today's kids be using a slang expression popular decades ago?

An old-model maroon car behind them ran the Oakland Boulevard light, then immediately slowed down. Since you can't pass on A1A, what was the driver's hurry? If the idea wasn't so paranoid, Kate would swear they were being followed by a rank amateur.

When Marlene turned right to take the Sunrise Bridge to the mainland, the old car turned, too. Kate tried to get a look at the driver, but the car had tinted windows. By the time they reached the hospital, Kate relaxed. The maroon car was no longer on their tail.

Though they had to park yards away from the entrance, Kate and Marlene walked into the lobby in good spirits. Billy's rambling reportage of the tango lesson and how Mary Frances's teacher had danced with him had kept them laughing.

The little boy seemed almost happy. Certainly happier than at any time since being separated from his mother. Kate accepted—and felt grateful—that the flaky ex-nun had been responsible for Billy's mood swing.

In the gift shop, after much discussion, Billy selected a pink rose in a glass vase for his mother. Then Kate and Marlene waited in the hall, giving Billy some alone time with his mother.

"Should I ask Donna about the cut-up negative I found in her wastebasket?" Kate worried that an innocent Donna might report her snooping to Nick Carbone and, maybe worse, ban her from seeing Billy. She had no idea how a guilty Donna might react.

"I thought we decided one of Whitey's final four visitors is our killer."

"Donna might have expunged herself from that list. And murdered her great-uncle to make sure the complete count never reached the police."

Marlene looked as if she needed a cigarette. Kate recognized her sister-in-law's Bette Davis–like nervous hand gestures that so perfectly mimicked smoking. "I bet great-uncle Carl put those pieces in the basket." Fire and Ice—painted fingernails flew past Kate's face.

"Why?"

"Well," Marlene floundered, "well, maybe to cover up evidence of animal abuse."

"It always comes back to that, doesn't it?" Kate stared at her own nails, unpainted, and in desperate need of TLC. "Carl could have been covering up Donna's elephant abuse, right?"

"Okay. Let's go in and talk to her before Nick Carbone or one of his men show up."

Kate scrambled through her big, black linen bag for a Pepcid AC.

"Mrs. K, Mommy says I can print my name on her cast." Billy waved a Magic Marker at Kate. "The nurse gave me this. You and Marlene can autogwaph her leg, too. That's what it's called."

Donna, smiling through gritted teeth, said. "Don't press too hard, Billy."

"Are you sure you should be doing this?" Kate tried to keep total disapproval out of her voice.

"Yes, don't worry." Donna nodded at Billy. "Since I'm going to be wearing this sucker for a long time, I want my big boy's name on it."

Each, in turn—Kate steadying Billy's hand—autographed the cast, gently, and in silence. There was, indeed, a sense of ritual about the "signing ceremony" as Donna called it.

Marlene placed the Magic Marker on the bedside table, and Donna nodded again. "Good." She sounded pleased, as she focused on Kate. "Mrs. Kennedy, they won't tell me when I can go home. Billy goes back to school on Monday. Can you keep him till then?"

Even if the child weren't there, looking up at Kate with those big blue eyes, she'd have said yes.

"I'll try to make other arrangements for next week." Donna's voice broke.

"No." Billy moved from his mother's bed rail to Kate's side. "Why can't you come home, Mommy?"

147

Kate put her arm around Billy. "Your mommy will be coming home soon, darling. You'll stay with me until she does."

"Promise?" Billy asked, eyes filling with tears.

"I promise." *And now your ersatz grandmother is going to interrogate your bedridden mother. Nice family values, Kate.*

"Billy, why don't you and I go down to the lobby? I saw an ambulance in the gift shop that I want to show you." Marlene sounded confident her bribe would work.

"I like frucks, not ambulances." Billy wasn't so easily bribed. "And I want to stay with my mommy."

"This one has a really loud siren." Marlene upped the ante.

"Go ahead, Billy." Donna said, "Mrs. Kennedy and I have some stuff to sort out."

When they'd gone, Kate wasted no time. She had to know. "In your apartment yesterday, I noticed cut-up pieces of a negative in your wastebasket."

"Doing a little snooping, were you?" Donna looked and sounded defiant.

"Someone murdered Whitey and Carl. Photographs showing elephant abuse could have been the motive for Whitey's death and, indirectly, for Carl's. So, yes, I snooped."

"As fond as you are of my boy, Mrs. Kennedy, it must be tough believing his mother's a murderer."

Kate met and held Donna's cold, dark eyes. "I'm praying she's not."

Donna blinked first. "While you were rummaging around my apartment, did you find a clipping from the *New York Times*?"

It was Kate's turn to blink; she could feel her face flush.

"So, were you surprised that I read the *Times*, Mrs. Kennedy? Or just surprised that I wanted to learn more about the nationwide abuse of circus animals?"

Kate's stomach burned. "I think you wanted to discover how much the *Times*' writer knew about elephant abuse in the Cunningham Circus."

"You would think that, wouldn't you, Mrs. Kennedy? Your kind always thinks the worst of my kind."

"Now, just a minute, young lady."

"I'm no lady, and we both know it. But that doesn't mean I have no morals. Women like you get that mixed up, Mrs. Kennedy." Donna's voice was both hoarse and harsh.

Kate, stunned into silence, backed away from the bed.

"Did it ever occur to you that I wanted to help the *Times* editor expose Sean Cunningham's dirty little secret? Or that I wanted to force Sean to admit some slimeball in our circus was abusing Edgar? Or that, for God's sake, I was the one who posed the elephants for Freddie's photographs?"

Twenty-seven

If Marlene asked one more time, "What's wrong?," a question Kate couldn't even begin to answer with Donna's son clutching her hand, she'd scream.

"Ixnay." She tried Pig Latin, hoping Marlene might remember the word from a language they'd learned as preteens, used briefly—so proud to have broken Kate's mother and father's secret code that had shielded the girls from unsuitable adult conversation—and then, for the most part, had forgotten.

Would she ever get out of this lobby? Or was she damned to pace its tile floor like the dead paced the deck on Charon's ferry as they crossed the river Styx? Would Broward General Hospital become her own personal purgatory? Kate, the penitent, confessed. Mea culpa, mea culpa: Guilty as Donna charged. She was a judgmental old snob. How much time would she have to serve?

Nick Carbone, leaning heavily on a cane, limped toward them.

"Good God, Kate, you're pale as a corpse. And who the hell is ixnay?" Marlene sounded frightened. "South Florida is still part of America, you don't have to talk to Carbone if you don't want to."

"Not who. What." With her free hand, Kate rubbed her forehead, sweaty despite the air-conditioning. "Ixnay is Pig Latin for nix."

Marlene just stared at her.

Kate released Billy's hand. "Nick is the least of my problems. Take Billy to the car. Let him play with his new ambulance. I'll meet you there."

Nick Carbone was close enough to touch.

She held her head high, nodded in Nick's direction, then whispered one final order to Marlene. "Please, go. I can't answer any questions now. Not yours. Not his. Not even my own. Don't worry. I'll get rid of Nick."

"You will, huh?" Nothing wrong with the detective's hearing.

Minus a mirror, Kate couldn't be sure, but Nick had to look worse than she did. Murder had an aging effect, especially for those trying to catch a killer. Her guilt-filled heart found room to pity her fellow investigator.

"What can I do for you, Nick?" Pleasant. Polite. Collegial.

"For starters, you can tell me why you tampered with evidence in Donna Viera's apartment."

Not purgatory. Hell. No reprieve. The souls in purgatory eventually got out. In hell, the sentence, eternal damnation, had no possibility of parole. "Why would you say a thing like that?" Kate tried a defensive tactic . . . and not a very good one.

"Please drop by the Palmetto Beach police station this afternoon, Kate." Pleasant. Polite. Collegial.

"Why?" She came across as much bolder than she felt.

"To have your fingerprints taken. We'd like to see if they match the prints on several pieces of a negative found in the Viera apartment."

"Well, well, hello, Mrs. Kennedy." Sean Cunningham had slithered up to them unnoticed. Freshly bathed and dressed in a white shirt and crisp khakis, the man still appeared rancid.

"Fancy running into you, Kate. Visiting our Donna, are you?" Linda, in fiery red Capri pants and a matching tube top, carried a huge bouquet of orchids and a small doll dressed in a replica of Donna's blue, drum majorette costume. She tossed her blonde curls, turned away from Kate, and pointed a red-tipped finger at Nick's cane. "Are you a patient here, too, Detective?"

"Just leaving." Nick sounded strained, and Kate could see he was in pain. "Since you and I have an appointment at six, Mrs. Rutledge, I'll see you later."

"Now I trust you won't be keeping Linda at the police station too long, Detective." Sean favored Carbone with his broad clown smile. "I'm holding a wee wake for Whitey, tonight at seven, and I wouldn't want one of the loves of his life to be missing it."

"At your place?" Nick asked. "I might drop by."

Sean nodded, his smile shrinking to a grimace.

As Nick hobbled off, he almost bumped into Suzanna and Olivia Jordan, who'd just arrived.

Hail, hail, the gang's all here. Broward General Hospital's lobby: crossroads of murder suspects. How Kate would love to know which of the four had electrocuted Whitey, planted the smoke bombs, and shot Carl and Freddie.

Sean seemed the most obvious candidate for the last two murders. He'd been in the circus for the entire matinee and only exited after the firemen had discovered Carl's body.

Though a prime suspect for Whitey's murder, Linda seemed to be out of contention for the flea market murders. She'd been in the corridor with Marlene when the smoke bombs were planted in the circus. Of course, she could have had an accomplice. Why would an innocent woman have lied to Marlene about her past?

Suzanna never had returned to the corridor after her scene with Freddie. Where had she been? Planting smoke bombs? Shooting Carl and Freddie? Kate appraised Suzanna's cool beauty as she greeted Sean and Linda, who were getting visitors' passes at the reception desk. Was Mama Jordan capable of triple murder? To protect her daughter from Whitey? From Freddie's blackmail? And could Suzanna and Whitey have been involved? Not unlikely with this bunch. The man seemed to have slept his way through the corridor. *"Your kind always thinks the worst of my kind."* Donna's haunting words stung anew. Kate flushed, wanted to flee.

"You're leaving, Mrs. Kennedy?" Olivia asked in her soft voice, with its perfect diction.

Kate nodded. "Yes, Marlene and Billy are waiting outside."

"It's still only two visitors at a time," the receptionist said.

"First come, first served," Linda said. "Let's go see the patient, Sean."

The clown reached into his shirt pocket and handed

153

Kate a card. "My address. I'd like you and Marlene to join us for Whitey's wake. After all, you're part of our corridor family now."

Kate hoped her shiver didn't show. Repulsed or not, she wouldn't miss this wake if her life depended on it. She took the card. "Thanks. I'll be there."

Sean winked. "I knew you'd come." Before Kate could process his words, he spun around and stepped into the elevator, patting Linda's backside.

Olivia sighed. "He's a pig, Mrs. Kennedy. If Mom and I didn't need the corridor to make a decent living, I'd slit him up the middle, roast him on a spit, and feed him to the tigers."

Kate believed her. She also believed Olivia would have been more than capable of planting smoke bombs, shooting Carl and Freddie, and then returning to the corridor, pretending to be all upset by Freddie's black-mail letter. Disarming and shrewd. A dangerous combination.

And, unlike her mother, Olivia was hefty enough to have tossed Freddie's body into the feed bin.

The fresh air cleared Kate's head. She walked briskly through the parking area, thinking Marlene must be ready to retire from baby-sitting. As she drew closer to the Chevy convertible she noticed an old maroon car—a Ford, she thought—a row over. It looked a lot like the one that had appeared to be tailing them earlier. Strange. Had one of the four suspects arrived in that car? Maybe Marlene had spotted the driver.

Billy and Marlene were nowhere to be found. Kate felt a surge of panic, starting in her stomach and rising to her heart. Then she heard laughter.

"Kate!" Marlene called. "Over here."

Her sister-in-law's head popped up from behind a SUV the size of a New York City studio apartment. "We're playing hide and seek."

Kate walked around the vehicle's rear end. Marlene crouched behind the front wheel, wide enough to cover her considerable girth.

"Where's Billy?"

Marlene gave her one of those "how dumb can you be" looks. "If I'm hiding, Kate, obviously, he's seeking."

Panic took control. Kate screamed. "What's wrong with you, Marlene? There's a killer loose in the hospital, and you don't know where Billy is!"

"I found you, Marlene." Billy's head poked around the front of the car.

Five minutes later, Kate had apologized for overreacting, and Marlene had allowed that she might have been a tad cavalier.

Kate mentioned Donna's four visitors and that Nick had asked her to stop by the police station, but she couldn't share her feelings or suspicions with Billy in the backseat.

The boy chattered happily, repeating Kate's mantra. "Mommy will be home soon."

As they approached the sharp left turn off Sunrise on

to A1A, Marlene braked, but the car kept going, picking up speed, out of control. Missing a van full of teenagers heading south, they almost flew across the highway onto the beach and, for a brief moment, seemed to hover over the sand. Only then did Kate remember that she'd forgotten to ask Marlene and Billy about the maroon car and, worse, hadn't written down its license plate number.

The last thing she heard as her forehead hit the windshield was Billy screaming.

Twenty-eight

"It's only a goose egg, Marlene. For the last time, I'm not going to the emergency room." Kate pressed an ice bag to her forehead. "If I had my way, I'd never again step foot into Broward General, Palmetto Beach Medical Center or, for that matter, the Mayo Clinic."

Marlene and Kate were sitting on the off-white couch in Kate's off-white living room, furnished in pale neutrals by her son Peter's partner, a psychiatrist by profession, but an interior decorator by passion. Charlie, who'd died before they could move into the apartment, had taken one look at its decor and accused Edmund of being a closet color-phobic. With the couch now sporting the Westie's claw marks and dubious stains, Charlie would have felt more at home.

Billy and Ballou sat between them, the former very concerned about Kate's sore head, the latter seeming to sense his mistress needed the comfort of a close encounter with his white fur.

Late-afternoon sun streamed in through the balcony doors; its rays, like a washed-out rainbow, reflected in the coffee table's glass top.

Kate counted her blessings. Despite several sunbathers being startled out of their prone positions, no one, including the Chevy's three passengers, had been hurt.

As scantily clad teenagers gaped, one lithe blonde beauty had offered ice wrapped in a yellow polka-dot towel that matched her bikini. Then, smelling of suntan lotion and salt, she'd held the ice against Kate's head, her quick act of kindness preventing Kate's forehead from being even more swollen and black and blue.

Considering the careening car could have killed some of the sunbathers, the spring breakers had responded like angels of mercy. The Fort Lauderdale police hadn't been nearly as accommodating, asking lots of rude questions, and giving an indignant Marlene a sobriety test. Kate giggled nervously, wondering if they'd ask Marlene to walk a line drawn in the sand. Instead, Marlene had to bring her index finger to her nose and keep her balance while standing on one foot.

The police had given Marlene a citation for reckless driving, but as they were still nosing around, Marlene's mechanic from her gas station at the corner of A1A and Oakland Park Boulevard arrived and insisted that someone, maybe a vandal, had jimmied around with the brakes.

Not a vandal, Kate thought as she petted Ballou. A

killer. A killer who drove an old-model maroon car and who, bold as brass, had done his dirty work in the Broward General Hospital's parking lot. A killer who'd stalked them, then returned and seized the day while Marlene and Billy were off playing hide and seek.

A killer she would catch if—well—if it killed her.

"You're not going to the police station. I'm calling Nick Carbone now and canceling." Marlene stood.

"It's not a dentist appointment, you know, it's a command performance." Kate wondered what being fingerprinted would be like. Would she be treated like a criminal? She wasn't frightened. Not really. Just curious.

"I want to see the police cars." Billy made a screech-like siren sound, causing Ballou's ears to perk up. "Let's go, please, let's go."

Marlene had whipped out her cell phone. "Kate, your stomach must be in a knot and, forget about a goose egg, that bump on your forehead is the size of an ostrich egg. You should be in bed." She pressed some numbers. "Information, I need the Palmetto Beach Police Department's number, please."

Kate stood, too, hoping she wouldn't wobble. "You listen to me, Marlene. My decision is made. I'm going to take two Tylenol and a Pepcid AC, then I'm going to the police station to have my fingerprints taken. So now you decide. Do you want to stay here and watch Billy? Or do you both want to come with me?"

No contest. Marlene snapped her cell phone shut.

Kate sank down in the front passenger seat, trying to get

comfortable and feeling grateful that she wasn't behind the wheel. Since Marlene's car had been towed to the gas station for a complete overhaul, she'd offered to drive Kate's bland Chevy—a much newer model, but not nearly as much fun as Marlene's now laid-up vintage convertible.

In the backseat, Billy chattered about *Law & Order*, his favorite TV show. He knew all the main characters by name.

How late did Donna let the boy stay up? Kate checked her inner critic to make certain her judgment call hadn't been based on either elitism or class consciousness. Life as a recovering snob wasn't going to be easy.

The Neptune Boulevard Bridge was down, so in less than ten minutes they were turning north on Federal Highway.

The box-shaped, beige stucco, really ugly Palmetto Beach Police Department building shared a parking lot with Town Hall, another homely edifice. An edgy Kate found herself checking the lot for a maroon car. Someone had tried to kill them this afternoon. A totally cruel someone who'd been aware a small boy was in the car.

This wasn't Kate and Marlene's first visit to police headquarters. Nothing had changed. The grimy, gritty waiting room with its pale green walls and cheap rattan furniture still looked like a low-rent dentist's office, and the same handsome, young African-American policeman still manned the metal desk.

159

"Good afternoon, Mrs. Kennedy." He smiled, briefly. "And I see you have your sister with you."

"Sister-in-law, Officer." Kate smiled back.

"And the young man?"

"I'm Billy. Can I ride in a police car with a siren?"

"Well, I think we can arrange that." The policeman met Kate's eyes. She saw no warmth. "Mrs. Kennedy, I know that Detective Carbone wants to see you alone." He nodded at Marlene, then picked up the phone on his desk. "I'm calling our community relations director. She'll be happy to give this young man and your sister-in-law a nice, long ride in a patrol car."

"With a siren?" Billy's smile, the only genuine one in the waiting room, sparkled.

"Yes, a really loud siren." The policeman hit three numbers on his phone.

"Isn't that special?" Marlene didn't even attempt a smile. Her sneer said it all.

A curt Carbone greeted Kate. "Sit down, you look ill."

She bristled, but laughter quickly replaced anger. "Well, coming from a man who looks like death, I'll take that as a compliment."

He laughed with her.

"Listen, Nick, I admit I picked up the pieces of that negative in Donna's apartment. I'm guilty. Do I still have to be fingerprinted?" She could picture Charlie up in heaven, shaking his head and groaning.

"You confess to tampering with evidence." Did she only imagine a hint of amusement in his voice?

160

"I didn't tamper; I only touched, then left the pieces for the police to find."

"As a homicide detective's widow, you know better, Kate."

"Did you find the *Times* editorial?" She decided to tell all. Be up front. God, could she be in real trouble here? Did she need a lawyer? Her head hurt. Suddenly, a gentle breeze seemed to caress her lips. Charlie sending her a message to seal them?

"Anything else you'd like to confess to, Kate?"

"Look, I snooped, but that's all I found, and I left everything there for you."

"The Palmetto Beach Homicide Department will be eternally grateful." Nick sounded really angry.

"I'm in trouble, aren't I?"

He stood, leaning heavily on his cane. "You're in danger, too."

She bit her lip, afraid she'd cry. "You know about Marlene's car."

"Why don't you start at the beginning and tell me everything that's happened since you gals went to work at the flea market?" He phrased it as a question, but Kate recognized an order when she heard one.

She'd talk. But terrified as she felt, she realized—and resented—that Nick wouldn't share what he'd found out with her.

Twenty-nine

"And that miserable bas—er bum—Carbone took your fingerprints anyway?" Marlene sounded outraged.

"Well, not personally, but yes, one of his minions did." Kate took another swipe with a Wash 'n Dri at the ink staining her right thumb. "After I'd told him all—well, almost all—I knew, he told me my prints were needed for elimination. It seems that in addition to Donna's and mine, the police found yet another print on a piece of the negative."

"Freddie's." Marlene said. "He took the pictures, right?"

Kate shrugged. "But the police could easily get Freddie's and Carl's prints, they're both in the m-o-r-g-u-e." She spelled so Billy, the *Law & Order* fan, wouldn't understand.

"Okay, tell me the rest later." Marlene, no doubt dying of curiosity, had gotten the message.

Billy tapped Kate's shoulder. "You shoulda come with us, Mrs. K. We had the siren going and the big red light flashing."

"Sounds like fun. Where did you go, darling?" Kate twisted her neck to face Billy in the backseat, her goose egg throbbing as she turned.

"Around and around and around in circles in the parking lot." Billy said, then screeched out his siren sound. "Better than riding in a fire fruck, right, Marlene?"

"Better than any fruck." Marlene giggled.

Kate spun back around, giving Marlene a dirty look, and herself a huge headache.

Mary Frances, dressed to kill in a pale-blue satin sheath with a trumpet flare at the hemline and matching blue satin pumps, greeted them in the lobby.

"Don't you look lovely, Mary Frances," Kate said.

The dancing ex-nun's thirties movie star–style gown was—as Kate's granddaughter, Katharine, would say—awesome, complementing Mary Frances's red hair and creamy skin, not to mention her slim figure. But the Broward County tango champion's striking appearance boded no good. Kate had hoped to con Mary Frances into baby-sitting while she and Marlene went to the wake. Obviously, Mary Frances had other plans.

"I've been stood up."

Thank God!

Kate lowered her eyes, so Mary Frances couldn't see the window to her wicked soul. "What a shame. Who's the scoundrel? He doesn't know what he's missing."

"The Senior Ms. South Florida talent coordinator. He invited me for dinner and dancing at the Breakers, and he just now called to cancel." Mary Frances gestured with her tiny cell phone. "Had an attack of conscience. Said our dating would be a conflict of interest, and that he couldn't possibly jeopardize his integrity or his position in the contest. After I've been waiting for him in the lobby for fifteen minutes."

"Why?" Kate asked, thinking about how she could

suggest that Mary Frances spend the evening with a much younger man.

"Do tell all." Marlene was smirking.

Great. In about three seconds, Mary Frances, mad at Marlene, would storm off, and Kate would lose a sitter.

She had to act fast. "Well, you look so beautiful, Mary Frances, why don't you come up to my apartment, and I'll take some glam shots of you? Let's seize this . . . er . . . adversity and turn it into a photo op. You can use the pictures in your press kit." She hoped she had film in her camera.

Marlene opened her mouth, but before she could speak, Kate barked out an order. "You and Billy can take Ballou for a walk while I work with Mary Frances."

As Mary Frances placed her cell phone into an antique handbag, struggling with its tortoiseshell clasp, Kate raised an eyebrow at Marlene and gestured toward Billy, who was running his fire truck across Aphrodite's feet, splashing water all over the Ocean Vista lobby's tile floor.

Sixty years of shared nonverbal communication— used in church during weddings and funerals, at sick beds in hospital rooms, in libraries, at Broadway shows and double features, and in front of Kate's children—worked once again. Marlene, back in the game, nodded.

Mary Frances glanced into one of the lobby's many mirrors. "You're right, Kate. I look too good to just go home, wash off my face, and hang up my dancing shoes. Let's get up to your balcony before the sun sets."

"You should report that talent coordinator to the pageant committee and get him kicked out of his position." Marlene made "position" sound R-rated. "I'll bet you're not the only contestant he hit on." Her sister-in-law's smirk, now buried under the guise of sympathy, appeared more like a concerned grimace. Or at least, Kate hoped Mary Frances interpreted it as concern. Marlene—even when in on the game plan—never quite knew when to cease and desist.

At seven-thirty, with Billy bathed, fed, and dancing the tango with his baby-sitter—who after her glamour shots had gone up to her condo and changed into jeans and a T-shirt—Kate and Marlene were in the car on their way to Whitey's wake.

Posing Mary Frances, under Billy and Marlene's direction, had turned out to be a lot of fun. And if Mary Frances photographed half as good as she looked in the lens, she'd have some great shots.

Ballou had been walked and fed, too, and the humans had dined on pizza and an ice cream cake that Kate found in her freezer. She'd opened a bag of spinach greens, diced some celery, poured some vinaigrette on top, and served the salad to ease her conscience. Only Mary Frances had eaten any of it.

Kate's head ached and her stomach rumbled, but she felt the thrill of the hunt as they crossed over the Neptune Boulevard Bridge, heading into an evening of intrigue and possibly danger.

There would be plenty of time to talk; they had a long ride ahead of them.

Sean Cunningham lived way out west in one of the new, very expensive developments that had sprung up so far from the ocean that east-siders sneered, saying those people, who'd paid millions for mansions abutting the Everglades, could just as well have been living in Kansas . . . only without the threat of alligators crawling into their backyards.

"So what else did you and Carbone talk about, Kate?"

"First I told him about the mysterious maroon car, and he said he'd look into it." She rushed on, "Then I pretty much told him everything I know. Or, to be more accurate, suspect." Kate felt an irrational sense of betrayal, admitting this to Marlene. "He kept reminding me that I'd tampered with evidence. I felt frightened and figured I'd better come clean."

"What about him? Did the good detective share anything that you didn't already know?"

Kate heard criticism and sarcasm—and a seeming lack of empathy—in Marlene's question. "Actually, yes."

"Sorry, I know I'm impossible." Marlene reached over and patted Kate's hand. "Chalk it up to being tense and tired, not to mention frustrated."

"I told you, I'd drive." Kate's tone returned to neutral. She related to tense and tired.

"With that throbbing headache?" Marlene laughed. "No, thanks." She turned onto the ramp leading to 95 South. "So, tell me what Carbone said."

"When we discussed the four suspects—and Nick had zeroed in on the same quartet—he said they insisted all of them had been in Whitey's bathroom together."

"No!"

Kate nodded. "Yes. All of them swear they were squeezed into that tiny room, chatting away with Whitey, and when they left he was still alive, sipping his scotch. Of course, they're probably covering for each other."

Marlene giggled. "Rub a dub dub, four suspects in a tub."

"Not quite." Kate, picturing the scene, giggled, too. "But listen to this, it turns out Nick had interviewed Carl and heard about the photographs *before* Carl and Freddie were shot in the circus."

"Then why were they murdered?" Marlene answered her own question. "Maybe the killer didn't know the police had already spoken to Carl."

"Or maybe we're wrong. Maybe there's a completely different motive tying these three murders together."

Thirty

In South Florida, west was relative. Kate figured these differences of geographical opinions—as with real estate purchases—were all about location, location, location.

Shelf dwellers in condos with ocean views deemed anywhere west of Federal Highway to be hotter, buggier, and far less desirable turf. To those on the beach, Margate, Coconut Creek, and Wilton Manors were *out* west. The recent real estate development beyond Coral Springs and Plantation was considered to be *way out* west. And bizarre. Why would anyone *choose* to live so far inland?

After all, the beach snobs reasoned, hadn't the Kennedy clan, Marjorie Merriweather Post, and Versace opted to overlook the sea?

Many A1A residents, including, on occasion, Marlene and Kate, sat in the sand and scoffed at the sprawling, yet confined, gated communities—especially the ones featuring golf courses, Olympic-size swimming pools, and clubhouses with social directors organizing 24/7 activities—categorizing them as regimented and parochial. Like summer camp for seniors.

Flying in the face of those east-siders' opinions, dozens of less expensive communities, dating back to the sixties—eons ago in Florida's history—had been home to happily retired New Yorkers for decades.

Today, western property—hot, buggy, and *really* far removed from the ocean—seemed to be in vogue. South Florida's frontier once had boundaries. No more. Developers beckoned, "Westward Ho!" And buyers, driving Mercedes SUVs, kept coming.

Unincorporated Broward County stretched almost to the Everglades. What the county's old-timers—part of that increasingly rare breed of South Florida natives— thought of as swampland had morphed into highly desirable communities, complete with man-made lakes, imported trees, and enormous homes, with prices starting at well over a million dollars.

In the spanking-new development of Westfield Pines, a filled-in marsh more than a forty-five-minute ride from the A1A, Kate and Marlene pulled into a winding, Royal Palm–lined driveway leading up to one of those mini-mansions.

"Well, we sure as hell had enough time to plan our strategy, didn't we?" Marlene put on the brake.

A smiling parking attendant opened her door. A second solicitous young man helped Kate out of the front passenger seat, grabbing hold of her elbow. "Watch your step, ma'am. These slates can be slippery."

They stepped into a buzz of mosquitoes, swarming in the thick, muggy, jasmine-sweet air.

Tempted to yank her elbow out of the young man's hand, Kate felt achy and ancient, sure she must look every bit as bad as she felt.

A smooth baritone voice, backed by a band, and singing "When I Fall in Love," jarred her. Decades ago, she and Charlie had co-opted those lyrics and turned them into their anthem.

She missed a step. Embarrassed, she mumbled, "Sorry," then wondered if she was apologizing for being old.

Not a very promising start to an evening of detective work.

Kate straightened her back and lifted her chin, forcing a smile. She'd allowed herself twenty minutes and, despite her sore head, worked fast, putting on makeup and pressing her blue silk pants suit. By God, she wasn't about to let all that effort go to waste.

"Welcome to my *casa*." Sean, in a Gatsby-era navy blazer and white lightweight wool trousers, loomed in the open front door. He held a highball glass in one hand and listed tipsily to the left. Sweat glistened on his brow, droplets dribbling down into the creases in his jowls.

Great. Greeted by a half-drunken host before the wake had gotten underway.

"What an interesting house, Sean." Kate laced her voice with enthusiasm. Marlene, right behind her, gasped, no doubt to swallow a giggle.

The huge U-shaped ranch, purple with lavender trim, and covered in twinkling lights, had to be the ugliest house in South Florida. Given the competition, no small distinction.

"Follow me, girls." Sean kissed Kate's cheek then reached for Marlene's. "Everyone's out in the piazza."

As he led them across a gilded foyer, its red velvet walls lined with portraits of circus clowns, to sliding glass doors, Kate yanked a Wash 'n Dri out of her purse and swiped her cheek.

They entered a festive courtyard, flanked on either side by the U-shaped building's wings that stretched down to a teak dock abutting one of those much-maligned man-made lakes. A white yawl—Kate figured it had to be a thirty-six-footer—was moored there.

In the piazza—designed to look like a center ring,

complete with a striped canvas top—buffet stations laden with ham, turkey, roast beef, and salads of every kind were manned by skilled waiters dressed like clowns. Kate spotted two very busy bars.

"'It's only a paper moon, sailing over a cardboard sea.'" Jocko, in his clown suit, and part of a six-piece band off to one side, couldn't have chosen more appropriate lyrics. Who knew the clown could sing?

Holding a wake in this circuslike atmosphere repulsed Kate, but hers appeared to be a minority opinion. The other mourners acted as if they were having the time of their lives.

"Happy hunting," Marlene said, then walked away.

They'd decided to divide and conquer. Since Marlene had already had a go at Linda, Kate would take on the doll lady tonight. Would Linda stick to her lies or change her tune and tell the truth? Unless she'd worked with an accomplice, Linda had Marlene, herself, as an alibi for Carl and Freddie's murders. So why had she lied about her past?

Marlene would tackle Suzanna Jordan and her darling daughter, Olivia. She'd accepted that assignment with relish, saying, "I want to check out Olivia's widely rumored romance with Whitey. If it was more than just a crush, the girl could have motives for all the murders, especially Freddie's. Maybe her icy mother might have melted and murdered all three men to protect her daughter. God, Kate, don't you love a mystery?"

Kate did, indeed, though she shuddered at the thought that tonight Sean Cunningham was all hers.

And her conversation with Nick continued to nag. Why would four people who didn't even like each other lie for each other? Unless. Her stomach jumped. Could it be a conspiracy?

"A peanut for your thoughts, Kate." Sean grabbed her wrist with a damp hand. "May I have this waltz?"

Dancing with the devil might be more than she'd bargained for, but Kate swallowed bile and stepped into Sean's arms.

As they took their first spin, she realized the band was playing "The Merry Widow Waltz."

Sean leaned in, his breath stale and smoky, and whispered, "I'm dying to know, have you figured out whodunit, Kate?"

Thirty-one

Marlene cornered Suzanna in the ladies' room. A most impressive loo, located off the courtyard in the right wing of the U-shaped house. It reminded Marlene of the elegant ladies' room in the Waldorf Astoria, which she'd ranked number one in New York City, after the Plaza moved theirs so far away from the main lobby that no lady could find it. The Algonquin—though, God knows, getting down those narrow stairs became more of a challenge each year—Saks Fifth Avenue, and Lord and Taylor's completed her list of the best public bathrooms in midtown Manhattan.

While Marlene hated to credit Sean with even a modicum of good taste, someone had designed a classy john for Chez Cunningham. The loo held four stalls with cherry-wood doors, each equipped with its own sink, flattering pink lighting, and an excellent supply of toiletries.

Feeling as if mosquitoes had invaded her French twist and flown down the deep vee neckline of her magenta crepe A-line dress, she'd fled to the ladies' room to brush away bugs and to repair and respray her platinum twist.

She had the damage under control and was sitting in a comfortable club chair before returning to the creepy wake, when a stall door opened and Suzanna exited.

The cool brunette nodded, saying, "Hello," then turned away to appraise herself in a full-length brass mirror.

Marlene thought, what's not to like? Suzanna exuded more class than the ladies' room. A tall, lean body, tight stomach, and compact butt. Plus Audrey Hepburn's cheekbones and her great hair style from *Wait Until Dark*. As usual, Mama Jordan was dressed simply— and expensively—in a white silk shirt and crisp black linen trousers. How come the heat and the bugs hadn't wilted Suzanna? Were women like her sweat-proof?

Jealousy made Marlene go for the jugular. "Tell me, Suzanna, do you believe that business with your brakes was an attempt to murder you? That you were meant to be the killer's first victim?" She sounded like a soap opera drama queen, but couldn't contain herself. "Who tampered with your car? Who wanted you dead? If you can answer that question, we'd know who the killer is,

173

wouldn't we?" Sometimes Marlene hated herself, but this was kind of fun.

Suzanna spun around, eyes wide. "Are you suggesting a serial killer?" Could that indignation be hiding fear?

Marlene took guilty pleasure in commanding the woman's full attention. And she suspected Suzanna had considered and rejected a serial killer theory long before this. Maybe the ice queen had jimmied her own brakes to set herself up as a victim, then went on to murder Whitey, Carl, and Freddie.

Suzanna sank into a matching club chair across the lounge from Marlene's. "You could be right."

Marlene, unprepared for agreement and having no clue where Suzanna was heading, said nothing.

"Whitey checked out those brakes himself, and concluded they'd been tampered with, that someone had wanted me or Olivia dead. My daughter often drove my car, you know." Sincere. Eager to share. Concerned, but not frightened. A brave mother protecting her daughter? A brazen murderer protecting herself?

"A serial killer?" Marlene spoke before editing.

Suzanna shrugged. A graceful gesture. "Maybe. Or perhaps the killer only wanted me or my poor Olivia dead—though I can't fathom why—but then, in a kind of domino effect, had to get rid of Whitey, Carl, and Freddie because each of them had learned his identity."

Marlene caught the masculine pronoun. She pictured a glass ball containing a winter scene with small figures in holiday attire gathered in front of a miniature house.

A ball that filled with snowflakes when you shook it. Not many of those for sale in South Florida, but Suzanna's snow job would blanket one of those balls like the blizzard of '47.

"Perhaps." Marlene agreed, keeping a straight face.

"A crazy person," Suzanna said, warming up to her theory, transparently pleased to be sharing her conclusions with Marlene.

"Why a crazy person?"

Suzanna's mouth formed an O, and she raised her brows. "Well, the killer must be crazy, Marlene. Why would a sane person want to harm either me or my daughter?"

"So we're looking for a madman?" Marlene prodded. "Anyone we know?"

"I've heard enough." A startled Marlene swung her head around in time to see the door to the last stall open. Linda stormed out, waving a roll of toilet paper. "You two playing cat and mouse have my knickers in a twist and my bowels in an uproar."

Suzanna gasped. "You witch, always sneaking around, spying on us." Marlene felt like a tennis spectator, her neck swinging from Linda to Suzanna. The latter had gone pale. Her posture-perfect shoulders sagged.

"If you and your frump of a daughter weren't up to no good, you wouldn't care who spied on you. Not that I ever did such a thing, you snooty, over-the-hill broad." Linda threw the roll of toilet paper. It flew like a football past three stalls, into the lounge, and smacked the right side of Suzanna's head. "Used to play darts. I once won in the local pub's women's division. Still have great aim, don't I?"

Suzanna screamed, then flung her purse. It fell far short of its target, who chortled. "Missed by a mile. No muscle left in that skinny old arm."

Jeez! Shades of *The Women*. This was too much. Marlene moved in between them. "Ladies, please."

"That British tart slept her way through two countries. When Whitey dumped her, she freaked out." Suzanna screeched like a shrew. A vein throbbing in her forehead appeared ready to pop. All resemblance to Audrey Hepburn had vanished. "You sneaked back in, didn't you, Linda? After we'd all left the bathroom, you returned, knowing he was drunk, and you killed my poor Whitey."

Damn! So they'd all been in the bathroom while Whitey soaked in his tub for the last time. Marlene, no prude, felt queasy.

"He wasn't your Whitey, ducks. He always loved me. You were just one of his diversions. Like your daughter, Olivia." Linda's laugh was cruel. "Maybe you're the one who came back. You had a key, did you? We'll never know for sure how you got in, will we? You shot Carl because he'd witnessed you going back in, or spotted you coming out for a second time, after you'd killed Whitey."

"You're mad!" Suzanna, stronger than she looked, shoved Marlene out of her way.

"And you killed Freddie because photographs don't

lie." Linda sounded triumphant. "His evidence would have sent your bony bum to death row."

Thirty-two

Kate danced back a step so she could meet Sean's olive eyes. "I've narrowed down the suspects."

He tightened his grip on her waist. Conscious of the less-than-firm skin in her midsection—too many bagels with cream cheese and not enough sit-ups—she decided she didn't care what Creepy Cunningham thought, then realized she didn't give a fig what any man thought. The resulting sense of freedom made her laugh.

"Something strike you as funny, Kate?" Sean shook his jowls. "Triple murder is nothing to laugh about."

"Just rejoicing in newfound freedom." Kate grinned, feeling good about herself.

"You're a strange woman." Sean's words wavered between flirtation and fear.

She nudged him in the right direction. "You're in the top four."

Jocko sang, " 'Waltz me lightly, hold me tightly.' " A smooth tenor baritone.

Sean stumbled and missed a beat, his heel coming down on her toe.

"Sorry, Kate," Sean said. "You startled me. Innocent men often react that way." She could feel his clammy hand through the silk fabric of her jacket. "Why do I deserve to be in your top four?" He tried a light touch, but sounded strained; his voice had lost its lilt.

"Oh . . ." She spun out, twirled, and returned to his arms. "Let me count the motives. To get your hands on photographs that would have confirmed suspected elephant abuse in the Cunningham Circus. To shut up Whitey, the man who'd called the Humane Society. To remove an eyewitness to Whitey's final visitors and the photographer who'd shot both the abuse pictures and those visitors."

Sean smelled of rancid sweat, and he was dancing faster than the music, spinning her in wider and wider circles.

"Let's move on to opportunity." Kate felt dizzy but confident and, as she spoke, her conviction that Sean had murdered the three men grew stronger. "You were at Whitey's on Sunday night, and you were in the circus yesterday afternoon when Carl and Freddie were shot."

"Don't bother with means, Kate. The police don't agree with you. Detective Carbone hasn't any evidence—or any reason—to arrest me." Sean spat as he spoke. "Indeed, quite the contrary. I've proven to the detective's satisfaction that I was never alone with Whitey on the night he died. Not even for a moment."

"Was it a conspiracy, Sean?" The words spilled out. "Like *Murder on the Orient Express*? Did all four of you plot to kill Whitey?"

Sean whirled her around so fast that she lost her balance. He lurched for her as she started to fall, keeping her upright, but twisting her elbow. "You look tired,

Kate. Why don't you go home, get into bed, and curl up with Agatha Christie?"

"May I cut in?" Nick tapped Sean's shoulder.

Kate hadn't seen Nick's approach, and his question made her partner squirm.

"Certainly," Sean said, as his wet jowls shook in a negative nod. "However, Mrs. Kennedy was just leaving."

She glared at Sean. "No, I'm not going anywhere. I have a few things I need to discuss with Detective Carbone." Giving Nick a weary smile, she moved out of Sean's arms and into his.

The band segued from waltz tempo to a fox trot, playing "The Second Time Around."

"Okay, Mrs. Kennedy, you never know when to quit, do you?" Nick's tone was critical, but she thought she saw a hint of admiration in his eyes. "So what do you need to discuss?"

He led well. Who'd have believed such a heavy man would be so light on his feet, especially after hurting his knee earlier that day?

"Sean thinks he's home free. That they all are. He's so smug, it's sickening. Nick, the four of them *were* in the bathroom with Whitey." Kate licked her lips, dry as the desert. She must look like death. "One must have come back, right?"

"It never occurred to you that I might have thought of that, Kate?"

"Well," she hesitated, embarrassed, then plunged on, ignoring his comment. "I . . . er . . . there's another possibilty. It could be a conspiracy. Maybe they all killed him."

His booming laughter caught her by surprise. "And maybe Sean's right. Maybe you should go home and curl up with Christie."

The teasing tone and its accompanying pat just below her waist reminded her of Charlie. She resisted a sudden impulse to kiss Nick's cheek. How tired was she? Had she lost her mind?

"What about the other two murders?" Nick asked. "Would they be part of this conspiracy theory?"

She shook her head. "I guess you're right. Every time I think I've figured something out, this mess moves in a new direction. It's just so frustrating."

"It's not your job, Kate."

"I need a drink." She wanted to get away from him, to go home and crawl into bed alone, and forget about her fleeting desire to kiss Nick Carbone.

He escorted her over to the closest bar, ordered her white wine, and said, "Drink up, find Marlene, and get out of this circus." Then he turned and walked away.

Kate downed half the wine in one gulp. It warmed her throat and would, no doubt, jump-start her acid reflux, but she didn't care, considering it medicine. As the alcohol soothed her nerves, she looked around the music-filled courtyard, searching for Marlene. A crowded dance floor, with many more guests sitting and eating at the round tables circling it, or standing three deep at the bars, chatting.

Where had Marlene gone? Should she be concerned?

Well, a killer was on the premises. Dancing, eating, chatting, or God forbid, alone somewhere with Marlene. Yes, damn it, she had reason to be worried.

"Mrs. Kennedy, have you seen my mother?" Olivia Jordan had been designated as one of Marlene's interviewees. The young woman sounded stressed and, putting worry on hold, Kate seized the moment.

"I was about to ask if you'd seen Marlene." Kate tried not to grimace as the wine turned to acid. "Maybe they're together." She hoped not. Or, if Marlene and Suzanna were together, she hoped they were still in the courtyard. Kate and Marlene had promised each other they wouldn't wander off with any of the four suspects.

"May I have a gin and tonic, please?" Olivia's soft, refined voice, with its prep-school diction, drew a prompt response from the bartender.

"Lemon or lime, Miss?"

"Neither, thanks." Olivia pushed thick dark hair away from her forehead. A pretty face, too seldom noticed because of her heavy body and shy manner. "I don't think they're together, Mrs. Kennedy. My mother can't stand your sister-in-law."

Some interviewer: Olivia had given Kate a perfect opening, but left her speechless.

"I didn't mean to offend you." Olivia laughed, as if that were exactly what she'd intended to do. "The list of people mother doesn't like is legion. Her competition in the corridor ranks among the top five." She flushed, giving her pale skin a pretty pink glow. "Of course, the murders have reduced the number of vendors on

181

mother's would-prefer-to-live-without list."

Kate gulped, but recovered her voice, and lobbed two questions. "How did you and your mother come to the corridor? Have you been selling there for a long time?"

"Over a decade. When I wasn't away at school, I spent all of my teenage and college years hawking Miriam Haskell jewelry." Olivia didn't try to hide her bitterness. "All the corridor vendors are—well, were— lifers."

"Do you know what made your mother choose the Cunningham corridor?" Kate persisted. "I think Suzanna would have had her choice of almost any location in the flea market."

"Mrs. Kennedy, why do you think that everyone would have wanted my mother? Because she was so beautiful or because she had those hot Haskell retro pins and earrings to sell?"

Smarting, Kate said, "A little of both, I guess."

"Truth is often a mixed bag, isn't it?" Olivia sighed. "Mother was a shoo-in for the corridor. She'd been sleeping with Sean Cunningham."

Kate felt her jaw drop.

"Their odd-couple romance bloomed for another ten years, until two months ago when my mother—and old enough to be his mother—fell in love with Whitey."

Thirty-three

"Kate, I need you in the ladies' room!" Marlene shouted from across the courtyard.

If she hadn't sounded so frazzled Kate might have ignored her. But her sister-in-law's words had drowned out the lyrics to "Stardust," and Olivia, now flushed and edgy, had clammed up, so Kate excused herself.

Inching her way through the dancers, Kate wondered why Olivia had blabbed the family secrets? Did she dislike her mother so much that she wanted to incriminate Suzanna? What other reason could Olivia have? Why would she air all their dirty laundry to Kate? Did Olivia know Kate and Marlene had not only been investigating the murder, but were down to four suspects? Could she be trying to give her mother a motive to obscure her own? And what about Sean? Olivia's spilling of the Jordan family's secrets gave him another motive in addition to covering up the elephant abuse: jealousy.

" 'Sometimes I sit and wonder why.' " Jocko's smooth refrain diverted Kate from murder.

The clown could sing. His rendition of Carmichael's classic made Kate feel as if he were singing to her alone. Every woman in the courtyard probably felt the same way. Kate glanced over to the bandstand. Jocko's droopy features reminded her of Emmett Kelly. Why did so many clowns look sad?

Thoroughly befuddled, Kate reached a disheveled

Marlene and followed her toward the ladies' room. As they passed by another bar, Marlene stopped and filled a napkin with ice cubes. When Kate gave her a puzzled look, she snapped, "Don't ask."

Linda, sporting a black eye and a ripped bodice, sat sobbing in a lounge chair in what Kate—if it weren't such a mess—would rate as a four-star ladies' room.

From a fetal position on the floor, a silent Suzanna gazed into space. The cool brunette's mascara had melted, not a pretty sight. Her refined features were streaked with blood. So was the wall behind her. "You're bleeding." Kate turned to Marlene. "Give me that ice."

"That's not blood. Linda threw a jar of liquid blush at Suzanna; it splattered." Marlene sounded fed up and a bit frightened. "Thank God, the jar was plastic, or we'd be picking pieces of glass out of that pretty puss."

Linda moaned and Marlene handed her the ice-filled napkin. "Here, hold this against your eye."

"What happened?" Kate stared at the seemingly shell-shocked Suzanna. "Why haven't you called a doctor?"

"Neither of the *ladies* wanted to go public." Marlene tittered. Kate recognized her laughter as a nervous reaction. "They had a catfight, each accusing the other of sneaking back into the bathroom and electrocuting Whitey. Seems he'd been romancing both Linda and Suzanna—not to mention Olivia."

"So I just heard." Kate sank into a chair, thinking how sleazy all the suspects were. How sleazy all the victims had been. "I need to go home, Marlene, my head hurts."

Marlene grabbed a paper cup from a dispenser, filled it with water from a cooler, rummaged through a silver tray on a counter, found a sample packet of aspirin, and handed the cup and the tablets to Kate. "Hang tight. We'll leave in a few minutes. I have a few questions for Lying Linda."

"I have nothing to say. Go home and leave us alone." Linda adjusted her ice pack.

"Now you listen up, Barbie Doll." Marlene loomed over Linda, sounding stern. "You either talk to me, or you and Suzanna's catfight and the Cunningham corridor's sexual swap shop will be the front-page story in the *Palmetto Beach Gazette.* My sister-in-law's a contributing editor."

Kate thought Marlene's less-than-truthful tactic would backfire. Linda struck her as the sort who'd prize any publicity, no matter how salacious.

"What do you want to know?" The doll lady sounded resigned. Kate had read her wrong. A lot of that had gone on tonight.

"Okay, for starters why did you lie about when and where you'd met Sean and Whitey?"

Suzanna groaned, then moved into a sitting position. Good. Kate had worried about her catatonic state.

Linda fumbled with her torn top, attempting to pull it together. "I figured if you knew the truth of my . . . er . . . my rather odd history with those blokes, you'd think I had a motive to kill Whitey."

"I already think that. Tell me." Marlene stood firm,

staring down at Linda's face.

"Back in my lap-dancing days at the Silver Swizzle, I fell in love with Whitey. I'd never met such an attractive, sexy man. Oh, neither of us had any illusions. I was determined to marry my millionaire, and Whitey was a practicing libertine. He never hid his promiscuity, but our affair lasted through my marriage and through all his women, right up to his last bubble bath."

"You tramp." Suzanna spoke in a hoarse, weak voice.

"What kind of blind fool are you?" Linda yelled. "Did you think you were going steady with Whitey? And you're no angel, either. You'd been sleeping with Sean for decades, but you cheated on him with Whitey, who wound up cheating on you with your own daughter. Now that's a bloody good motive, isn't it?"

"Shut up, Linda. You're betraying our pact." Suzanna sounded desperate.

"Every woman for herself, you skinny twit."

"I've heard enough." Marlene backed away from Linda. "Let's go, Kate. If they kill each other, the world might be a better place."

Kate stood. "Do either of you ladies drive an old maroon car? Maybe a Ford?"

"You've seen my car," Linda said, looking at Marlene. "And, anyway, maroon isn't my color, and I wouldn't be caught dead driving a Ford."

"Why do you ask?" Suzanna tried to stand but staggered.

Kate reached to help Suzanna up.

"The only one I know who drives an old car is Jocko," Linda said. "A Toyota, I think, but it's definitely maroon."

Thirty-four

"When you called the corridor vendors 'an incestuous bunch,' I had no idea how right you were." As she spoke, Kate was dialing Nick on her cell phone, wanting to update him on Jocko and the maroon car. Depending on his response, she'd decide if she should fill him in on the rest of the evening's news.

"Hot and sticky as all hell out here, but the fresh air smells good, doesn't it?" Marlene took a deep breath and exhaled. "I'm breaking my lease tomorrow, Kate. I don't care if I lose money."

"Do you think the corridor will reopen?" Kate didn't. She wondered if the Cunningham Circus would survive, now that its owner—or, his brother—appeared to be the prime suspect in three murders.

"Don't know. Don't care. I'm outta there tomorrow." Marlene shook her head. "I feel dirty, like I need a bath." She laughed. "Strange, this mess started in Whitey's tub."

"No, Marlene, this mess started in Whitey's bed."

"Nick Carbone." He shouted into her ear as if he were answering the call from China, but Kate could see him, weaving his way through the dancers, heading toward them.

"Hi, it's Kate. I have some news for you."

"Where are you?"

"Look over the head of the blonde twisting in front of you. I'm about four feet away from her."

"Why haven't you left?"

Jeez Louise! She was tempted to respond: Because I'm doing your detective work. "Listen, we need to talk. Walk down to the dock. Marlene and I will meet you there."

Ten minutes later, after Nick had shared first, saying he'd checked on all the vendors' cars and discovered that Joseph Cunningham drove an old maroon Toyota, Kate had told him everything she knew.

Marlene had followed up with a vivid report on the carnage in the ladies' room. Carbone had a belly laugh over that.

Now the three of them were sitting on the edge of the teak dock, staring across the dark, motionless lake.

If there were a whiff of salt in the air, or a hint of a breeze off the water, the scene might have been reminiscent of Jay Gatsby staring across the Long Island Sound at the light on Daisy's pier. Instead, they sat in silence, being eaten alive by mosquitoes.

Nick broke it. "Kate, you never got the license number, so we can't prove the maroon car you spotted belonged to Jocko."

Kate nodded. "Right." Depressing. She felt as motionless as the water.

"What next?" Marlene wiped away the sweat under her bangs with a tissue.

"Go home," Nick said. "I'm running a background check on Jocko. We know he and Carl Krieg belonged to the local bund. Let's see what else will turn up."

Wondering why the Palmetto Beach Homicide Department hadn't already completed background checks on the entire circus staff, Kate bit her lip. Had Nick zeroed in too early, then focused only on Whitey's four final visitors? Charlie had never suffered from tunnel vision. He'd run the best homicide department in New York City. Though to be fair, up to a half hour ago, she'd espoused Nick's narrow view.

The light across the lake flickered, and Kate, energized by a spark of memory, jumped up. "We're perfectly safe. Jocko's still singing." The strains of "I'll Be Seeing You" drifted down to the dock. "We'll go home in a few minutes, Nick. I promise." She tapped Marlene's shoulder. "Come on, we have to find the tigers' trainer. Jim something. I need to ask him a question about Jocko."

Jim Day, a good-looking man in a safari jacket, sat at a table near the bandstand. A longhaired cat, tortoiseshell in color, and, Kate gathered, affectionate in nature, slept on his shoulders.

"Hi, I'm Kate Kennedy. This is my sister-in-law, Marlene Friedman. We work in the circus corridor."

"Nice to meet you." Day stood to shake hands. "I noticed you ladies with Donna's little boy yesterday after I'd left the Big Top."

The cat leaped into an empty chair.

"This is Fluffy," Day said. "I never leave home without her."

"Linda will be so jealous. She didn't bring Precious." Marlene oozed charm, responding in flirtation mode, her hormones on automatic pilot. Handsome guy in the radar.

"What breed is Fluffy?" Kate asked, anxious to question the trainer about Jocko, but not wanting to grill him without some small talk first.

He smiled. A proud father's smile. "Fluffy's a Siberian Persian, raised on people food and Russian TV. I needed a visa to get her out of Moscow."

"Did you live in Russia?" Marlene gushed.

"I doubt Fluffy was exposed to Russian television in Palmetto Beach, Marlene." Enough. Kate moved on. "Jim, I need to ask you something that could be very important."

"Sit down, ladies." He gestured to two empty chairs. "My wife has gone to the ladies' room."

As Marlene's face fell, Kate thought about Mrs. Day walking into that war zone. Had Linda and Suzanna retreated?

Jim sat, too. Seeming to sense her master was all business, Fluffy remained in her own chair, looking regal.

"It's about Jocko." Kate could swear she saw a flicker of distaste distort Jim's even features.

"What?" Jim sounded guarded, yet open. Could that be a tiger tamer's strength?

"Jocko told Marlene that he'd searched all over the

circus for you during the smoke-bomb scare, then helped you get the tigers into their portable cages. Is that true?"

The trainer's fair skin flushed. "Absolutely not. I remember every detail of yesterday afternoon. How the band played the code bars that signaled trouble in the Big Top. How frightened my cats were. How I wondered why there were no flames. But I assure you, Kate Kennedy, I never laid eyes on that clown."

"Thank you." Kate stood, ready to face the long ride home.

"Ladies and gentlemen, your attention, please." Sean Cunningham's lilt, back in bloom, boomed. "First, a round of applause for my brother, Jocko, the Dean Martin of Palmetto Beach." Kate felt it akin to sacrilege. Sean had debased her idol.

The crowd gave Jocko a standing ovation.

"I have a surprise for you. Tomorrow, the Cunningham Circus and the Cunningham corridor will be, at the police's request, closed." Some of his audience laughed at the way Sean had rolled out, "request."

"But in honor of our dead comrades, Whitey Ford, Carl Krieg, and Freddie Ducksworth, tomorrow we won't mourn or grieve. We'll celebrate their lives." Sean paused. "I've arranged for Marino's Carnival, the finest in our grand country, to grace the flea market. They're setting up in the field behind the circus as I speak."

His captive audience clapped and cheered.

"And every one of my Cunningham Circus

employees, from the roustabouts to the high-wire acts, will be receiving full pay to enjoy the greatest carnival on earth."

"Fat lot of good that will do us vendors." Linda's British accent came from behind Kate.

"I'll pay all the vendors an average day's take." Sean yelled back.

"Since three vendors have been murdered and I'm out of there, it won't cost Sean much, will it?" Marlene said.

"So bring the family, ride the Ferris wheel, eat cotton candy, play games of chance, take the wife through the Tunnel of Terror." Sean screeched to a close. "Come celebrate with the Cunninghams!"

Thirty-five

Kate stretched, willing herself awake.

Ballou ran from his basket to put his front legs on the bed and ask for a morning pat.

She'd gone to bed at midnight, slept like the dead until six, when, still drowsy, she got up to go to the bathroom. Crawling back under the covers, she ignored the rising sun playing peek-a-boo through the slats in her wooden blinds, and dozed off again.

She'd dreamed about Charlie cutting in on her and Nick. No dialogue accompanied the black-and-white images. The players' body language created lots of tension, though. Very forties noir. And, though Kate hated to admit it, rather titillating.

By seven, she'd hopped out of bed and was brushing her teeth.

She did her best thinking while doing her toilette. Flossing stimulated her creative juices. She felt surprisingly good for an old gal this morning, and though her skin seemed sallow, the bump on her forehead had vanished and her eyes were clear.

Kate applied super-greasy, great-smelling, tinted moisturizer in upward strokes. Her daughter-in-law, Jennifer, had given Kate "the very best product on the market," and its gold-rimmed container, alone, must have cost a small fortune. Pleased with the soft blush of color now perking up her face, Kate made a decision: She would bring Billy to the carnival, and she'd talk Marlene into coming with them.

Marlene had vetoed attending Sean's carnival last night. Since she was divorcing herself from the Cunningham Circus corridor, Marlene refused to support the clown's latest ego trip.

Kate believed, in the light of day and with the prospect of a murderer riding the Tilt-a-Whirl, Marlene would come to her senses and go along for the ride. She laughed, spilling about thirty dollars worth of greasy drops. When had she become the wacky one?

Her cell phone played the opening bars of "As Time Goes By." She wiped off her hands, ran, and pressed the TALK button before the caller was transferred to voice mail.

"Kate Kennedy."

"It's Nick, Kate."

Her dream, still vivid, colored her response. "Yes." Prissy, barely pleasant.

"Get up on the wrong side of the bed?"

Damn the man. "No. I was . . . er . . . busy. It's only seven-thirty, you know. What can I do for you, Nick?"

"I have an update on Jocko." Nick tried to keep his voice neutral, but she heard a hint of anger. Why couldn't they treat each other like adults? If not friends, at least like colleagues?

"Look, I'm sorry. I guess I . . ."

"It's okay, Kate." He laughed a little and then coughed. "Now, about the clown."

"Yes." She couldn't conceal her excitement.

"Seems Jocko had several careers before going into the family business. Tried his hand at boxing, then worked as a shoe salesman and, for awhile, in a local garage as an auto mechanic."

"My God!" Kate collapsed into the unmade bed, her legs dangling over the side. Ballou licked her bare feet.

The detective grunted and said, "Yeah."

"Jocko tampered with Suzanna's car, didn't he? And fixed the brakes on Marlene's Chevy. He could have killed Marlene and me. And Billy." Her heart wouldn't stop jumping.

"In theory. No hard proof, though."

"Are you going to arrest him?" Was Jocko a serial killer? Three vendors dead. Two attempted murders. Suzanna. And Marlene. Or was Kate Jocko's target? With Billy as residual damage? Buy why would Jocko want the vendors dead? Oh, God, maybe he shot

194

Freddie and Carl because they could prove his brother, Sean, murdered Whitey.

Carbone's words came over her thoughts. "We're still gathering evidence, Kate. We can't be certain the maroon car you spotted and Jocko's Toyota are one and the same."

"Of course it's the same car." She'd check out the Toyota in the flea market's parking lot this afternoon.

"You're staying home today, right?"

She sat up straight and crossed her fingers. "Right." Just what she used to do when Charlie tried to be over-protective.

"Come on, Ballou, let's go wake up Billy." Mary Frances reported that she and Billy had watched *The Sound of Music* till ten P.M. Some baby-sitter, allowing the boy to stay up so late.

Thirty minutes later, they were on the beach. Kate, as usual, followed Ballou's lead. She smiled as Billy ran along the water's edge kicking sand and dead crabs.

"We'll stop by the bakery and buy fresh crumb buns to bribe Auntie Marlene to come to the carnival." Planning a murder investigation shouldn't be so much fun, but Kate was enjoying it.

"And then we're going to see my mommy." Billy's blue eyes sparkled in the sunshine.

"Yes, darling." It would be a short visit.

"What's a carnival?"

"Rides and games and cotton candy on a stick. You're going to love it. There should be a carousel, and you can ride any horse you want."

Flashes of an empty lot in Queens being miraculously transformed overnight into a gaudy, exciting carnival shot through her mind. A skinny ten-year-old deemed too small to ride in the upside-down rotating airplane. The beefy operator's shout: "You might fall out, kid. You don't meet the size requirement." The embarrassment of leaving the line, while Marlene was allowed to board . . .

But mostly she remembered the magic. The thrill of anticipation, watching the workers set up. Bright lights on the Ferris wheel. The fun house.

She sensed, even as a child, that carnivals had a seedy side, but in the excitement of the moment, she never cared.

Every August for three days a vacant lot in her New York City neighborhood turned into a wonderland, and she loved it. The magic ended in the early fifties, when Donald Trump's father bought the lot and built Northridge, an uninspired apartment complex. Ah, but once there was a spot . . .

Kate felt a tug on her sleeve.

"Mrs. K, what's wrong?" Billy sounded alarmed.

Only then did she realize tears were rolling down her cheeks. Nostalgia can be a killer.

Marlene had been disgracefully easy to bribe. She wanted to cancel her lease today and ask the police if she could start bringing her flea market wares home. Kate suspected Marlene also wanted to ride the Ferris wheel, but was too stubborn to say so.

Sated with crumb buns and toting leftovers for Donna, they arrived at Broward General at eleven A.M., ahead of schedule. The carnival would open at noon.

Billy walked into the lobby, grumbling about leaving Ballou at home. No matter how many times Kate explained that the Westie couldn't come to the carnival, the boy balked.

"Now, knock it off, Billy," Marlene said, "or we'll drive back home and leave you there, too. I'll call Mary Frances right now and ask her to baby-sit."

Billy stared at Marlene, weighing her threat.

"Let's go see my mommy." The discussion was over.

Donna looked chipper and appeared to be in good humor. She reached over the bed rail and wrapped her left arm around Billy. He kissed her cheek.

"The doctors were in this morning." Donna smiled. "They seem optimistic that I'll be fine, though I have a long way to go. I can go back to working with elephants." Donna glanced at Kate. "I've had an offer from Ringling Brothers."

"What wonderful news," Kate said, and she meant it. As she spoke, she made a decision. "You focus on getting better, Donna, and while you're doing that, don't worry. I'll take care of Billy until you're on your feet again."

Donna reached across the rail to squeeze Kate's arm.

Ten minutes later, Donna kissed Billy good-bye. "Have

fun at the carnival and listen to Mrs. Kennedy." She turned to Kate. "Can I talk to you alone?"

Marlene grabbed Billy's hand. "We'll meet you in the lobby, Kate."

"Let me be blunt, Mrs. Kennedy."

As if she'd ever been anything else. "Of course," Kate said. Funny how good manners kick in by reflex.

"I love my elephants. I'd never abuse them or any animal. You saw a prod, Mrs. Kennedy, and not a painful one, I promise. I tend to act standoffish with women who . . . look, what I'm trying to say here is I'm sorry I was rude to you."

"Oh, Donna. It's okay." Kate took her hand. "I made a mistake." She smiled. "And please call me Kate."

An answering smile. "One more thing, Kate."

"Yes?"

"Watch out for Jocko. Did you know he used to be an elephant trainer? I'm sure he's the one who abused Edna and Edgar."

Thirty-six

Sean Cunningham's imported carnival had no magic, but the crowds queued up for its mediocre rides, greasy food, and games of chance were spending money as if under a spell.

No fool, the clown had figured, correctly, that the flea market shoppers, disappointed there wouldn't be a Big Top matinee, would flock to the carnival. And while the outing might have been "a gift" to Sean's circus performers and roustabouts, most of his employees appeared to be spending far more than a day's wages at the carnival.

The Poker Wheel of Fortune and the blackjack table had serious gamblers glued to their seats, while prospective players waited impatiently for the bettors to go broke.

Many of the circus workers had brought their children and were trying to impress the kids by winning stuffed animals. They stood in long lines for the chance to spend five dollars to shoot down moving ducks or land balls in tiny baskets. Kate calculated that a parent's investment to take a teddy bear home ran around seventy-five bucks.

All the booths, game tables, food carts, and amusement rides were operated by men and women dressed as clowns. A couple of them, who were moonlighting circus performers, waved at Billy. Sean's idea? What a scary thought. One of those clowns could be Jocko.

Kate had scoured the parking lots when they arrived, driving up and down each lane while a restless Billy whined in frustration. No sign of the maroon car. Finally, she gave up and parked.

Marlene hadn't had any better luck with the policemen guarding the circus corridor. They told her to come back late tomorrow. Her property would be released then. Probably just as well, Kate thought. Maybe her granddaughter, Katharine, could help her and Marlene pack it all up. For sure, Jocko wouldn't be helping them.

"Not like when we were kids, Kate?" Marlene gestured to a rickety Ferris wheel. "That ride has to be as old as we are."

Kate laughed. "We're the ones who've changed. The magic's missing. In our dotage, we're becoming cynical and cautious." She pointed to the Ferris wheel. "But you're right. It does look familiar."

"You're going for a ride, aren't you?" Marlene asked. "You haven't changed, Kate. You're every bit as crazy as you were in 1948."

"Can I go for a ride, too?" Billy pulled on Kate's arm. "Please?"

Kate couldn't believe that even *this* money-grabbing carnival would allow a five-year-old boy to ride the Ferris wheel.

"How about we start on the carousel, Billy?" She gestured toward the merry-go-round blasting out canned music.

"I'll buy the tickets." Marlene stepped into a long line. "You and Billy go pick your ponies, but with this crowd, you may have to settle for inside horses."

They waited through two full turns, Billy's eyes aglow with anticipation. As the primary-colored horses went round and round, Kate thought, not for the first time, how similar the music was to the waltzes played in ice skating rinks.

"I want that red one with the feather in his hair." Billy boarded and staked his claim. He mounted the horse with very little help from Kate. She'd stand and hold onto him during the ride.

Billy had other plans. "Get on the white horse next to me, Mrs. K."

"Let me help you up." A clown stood there collecting tickets.

Kate started, squelching a scream. The clown was Linda, not Jocko.

"Didn't mean to scare you, love. I'm helping Sean out. Not enough clowns to go around." Linda laughed at her own weak joke.

"Get on the horse, Mrs. K! I'm not a baby. I want to ride by myself."

"Okay, Billy. And yes, Linda, you can give me a hand." Kate straddled the horse, feeling like a kid.

Linda took Kate's tickets.

"Where's Jocko?" asked Kate.

"Hawking the Tunnel of Terror." Linda laughed. "Sean wanted to do that job himself, but Detective Carbone has requested his presence over in the leasing trailer. Between us gals, Kate, I wouldn't count on the circus corridor reopening. I think Sean killed them all. And I'm going to tell that copper what I know."

"What?" Kate called out as Linda hopped off.

The merry-go-round jerked, then began its circle. The music blared. Patti Page sang "The Tennessee Waltz."

When Kate and Billy dismounted, Linda had vanished. Another clown had relieved her.

Marlene and Kate approached every clown they passed. Every ticket-taking clown. Every clown behind a food cart. Every clown dealing a hand of poker. No Linda.

They split up, agreeing to canvass the carnival and meet at the carousel in a half hour.

Kate kept confronting clowns. At first intrigued, Billy soon grew bored.

"Look, Mrs. K," he said, pointing to the Tunnel of Terror. "Can we go on that? Please? Please? It's just like a ride I went on in Disney World." He smiled, his big blue eyes shining. "I don't want to talk to any more clowns."

Kate felt the same way. She glanced at her watch. They had fifteen minutes before their rendezvous with Marlene. The line was short, and there were several children his age waiting. It looked as if they all might get on the next time around.

Jocko, in costume, stood outside the ride, barking its praises, comparing its denizens to Casper the friendly ghost. The clown stood in full view of the passengers, directing them into the cars. With him hawking outside, Kate and Billy would be safe inside. And of course, Jocko had no idea that Kate knew about his maroon car.

She still paused. Was this a good idea? "Okay, Billy, let's go."

The Tunnel of Terror had ten individual open seats, painted black and shaped like bats. Each bat-seat had wings connected to overhead wires that moved it through the tunnel. A smiling Jocko helped Kate and Billy into the last seat.

"You're going to love this ride, Billy. You'll remember it for the rest of your life."

Though less friendly than Casper, the ride wasn't too

scary. It reminded Kate of a very dark Small World without the water or the cute kids singing. A couple of Oz-like witches, a few vampires dangling from the ceiling, smoke seeping up from the ground, eerie music, and images on the walls giving the illusion they were riding through a haunted house . . . complete with coffins used as coffee tables.

As their bat-car turned a corner into complete darkness, it stopped short. The other cars seemed to have moved on.

Kate could hear Jocko saying, "Sorry, folks, the Tunnel of Terror has had a glitch. We need to close the ride down for a few minutes." He sounded as if he shouted into a microphone, still outside the entrance.

"Is anyone in here with us?" No one answered.

Billy cuddled closer. Kate felt him tremble. For a moment, fury replaced fear.

"It's all right, darling. But we need to move fast." She wanted to get to the exit before Jocko entered the tunnel.

She stepped out of the car, holding Billy's hand. Pitch black. How could she do this? "Don't let go, sweetheart."

"I won't cry. My mommy says I'm a big boy."

Kate felt capable of murder.

Billy scrambled out of the bat-seat, managing to keep his hand in hers.

She inched her way forward, running her other hand along the car, feeling for the bat's nose. "Okay. We're heading for the exit."

Someone shone a flashlight in her face.

"Oh, no you're not, Mrs. Kennedy. You're not going anywhere."

Though blinded, she recognized Olivia Jordan's soft, perfect diction and smelled her flowery cologne. She felt the muzzle of a small gun in her left side.

Kate blinked, moving her eyes away from the light.

"I don't like this ride," Billy said. "Let's go home."

Had anyone seen them come in here? Was Marlene looking for them?

Since Kate couldn't see Olivia, she had to keep her talking.

"It was all about your mother, right?" Kate spoke with authority, suddenly certain of what she said. "Whitey realized you'd tried to kill Suzanna. That you had Jocko fix her brakes. So after the four of you left Sunday night, you returned to Whitey's bathroom and killed him."

"You're a nosy old biddy, Mrs. Kennedy."

"Then you had to kill Freddie and Carl. They could prove you went back, couldn't they?" Kate stopped, feeling the gun against her ribs. "Or did Jocko shoot them for you?"

Olivia's hand, its finger probably on the trigger, shook.

"Are you okay?" a young male voice asked. Another flashlight shone in Kate's face. "We were in the car in front of you. We were worried when you and the kid didn't come out."

"Run, Billy, run straight ahead!" She let go of the

boy's hand and pushed him forward. "Run toward the man."

Olivia staggered as the man's flashlight moved over her face. Her flashlight fell to the ground.

Kate swung from the right and punched Olivia in the face, hearing her nose crack.

The gun went off.

Epilogue

They sat in the shade of a gaudy umbrella at a round table outside the flea market bakery. Billy, resilient in the way that only small children can be, was eating a jelly doughnut and sported a milk mustache.

While Marlene and Kate talked, Linda and Billy played Go Fish.

Marlene said, "Billy believes everything that happened was part of the Tunnel of Terror ride. He told me he'll never go on it again."

"Neither will I." Kate thought about the bullet hole in her silver belt buckle. The belt had been bagged as evidence. She hoped her slacks would stay up.

"Okay, Jocko had a major crush on Olivia. When she decided to get rid of her mother, he did the dirty work, right?" Marlene took a bite of her own jelly doughnut.

"Why did Olivia kill Whitey?" Linda looked up from her cards.

Kate shook her head. "Based on what I heard Olivia tell Nick, Whitey discovered she'd tried to murder her mother, and during their pre-pillow talk—Olivia never did get him into bed—he let that slip. So she killed him."

Linda sighed. "Something Sean said convinced me he'd killed Whitey to prevent him from exposing Jocko's animal abuse. That's what I wanted to tell Detective Carbone today."

"Who shot Carl and Freddie?" Marlene drained her coffee cup and reached for another doughnut.

"Jocko. For a price. Olivia had agreed to marry him." Kate hardly believed her own words. "Carl was killed because, though confused, he'd told Olivia about seeing her leave twice."

"What about Freddie? Was it because of those photographs that could prove when the suspects came and went?" Linda ignored Billy's "Go fish."

"No, no, he'd been long gone before Olivia's second time around. And the compromising shot of her and Whitey wasn't a motive, either. Olivia said she'd have been proud to show that photo to the entire world."

"Then why was Freddie murdered?" Marlene was losing patience.

"Because he stumbled on Jocko shooting Carl in the sword swallower's bed," Kate said.

"So the animal abuse and its coverup had nothing to do with the murders?" Linda asked.

"No. But animal abuse charges have been filed against Jocko and Sean. The Cunninghams are out of business. The Palmetto Beach Flea Market no longer has a circus."

"What about the animals?" Billy looked anxious.

Linda smiled. "I'll buy the circus. Precious and I like it here. I'll even let Suzanna work in the corridor. And of course, you ladies will always have a spot. Billy, too."

Billy waved his cards at Linda. "I win."

Center Point Publishing
600 Brooks Road ● PO Box 1
Thorndike ME 04986-0001 USA

(207) 568-3717

US & Canada:
1 800 929-9108